Battle for the Cure

Susan Larned Womble

Published by Page Pond Press
www.pagepondpress.com

This book is a work of fiction. Names, characters, places, and incidents are either the product of the author's imagination or are used fictitiously. Any resemblance to actual persons, living or dead, or to actual events or locales is entirely coincidental.

Inquiries should be addressed to: Page Pond Press at
www.pagepondpress.com email: pagepondpress1@gmail.com

ISBN: **00991397797**

ISBN-13: 9780991397792
First Edition

Printed in the United States of America
Copyright © 2015 Susan Larned Womble

ISBN: **00991397797**
ISBN-13: 9780991397792

DEDICATION

For Harper

Battle for the Cure

Susan Larned Womble

Published by Page Pond Press

ACKNOWLEDGMENTS

I would like to acknowledge my family, my husband, Gregg, my partner for all of life's adventures, my children Thomas and Amanda, my sweet granddaughter, Harper, my father, Tommy Larned, and my sister, Judi Taylor. I would also like to thank my writing critique group: especially Hannah Mahler, Rhett DeVane, Peggy Kassess, and Donna Meredith. They help with every aspect of the writing process and keep me on track. I would also like to thank my St. George retreat-writing buddies, especially our fearless leader, Adrian Fogelin and our organizer, Perky Granger for all of their guidance and fun times every year. I would also like to thank Paula Kiger, my editor. I would also like to thank the teachers of Hohenfels, Germany along with the people of Bavaria and Europe for the wonderful experience of learning about their culture as I travelled throughout Europe.

Chapter 1

After the last few months of being in constant danger, I'm ready to relax.

My self-assigned bodyguards, Eddie and Baako, accompany me back to my Bavarian farm. The rolling hills and green meadows remind me of my childhood. I roll the bullet molded into a four-leaf clover in my hand. I love that Riley gave it to me. I think of him saying, "something bad into something good." What a lucky charm it has turned out to be.

I miss Riley.

If it wasn't for this virus, if it wasn't for the quarantine, if it wasn't for the human trafficking and dictatorship and Merc murders, I might have a chance at a regular life, a relationship with Riley. But not now,

I'm fighting a war. A war for democracy, a free way of life.

As we reach the outskirts of my farm, I spot it, the magnificent metal giant, my Ferris wheel. Left over from a long forgotten carnival that blew through town many years ago, the rusty, dilapidated wheel remains workable, albeit tarnished and sluggish. A few of our army of children are still housed here.

Wish I could ride now, but out of respect, I first visit the graves of the Undesirables and the Uncounteds who died on this farm saving these children. It seems weird to be able to travel through our lands unencumbered. Fear of a reoccurrence of the virus has put the entire world back into a self-imposed quarantine. But not us rebels, we know the truth.

Much work still to do. We must overthrow the regime and save the princess and prince from the bloodthirsty King Emperor Merc, Richard the Great. What a joke! He is not great at all. Pure evil. I worry he will murder the queen and her heirs. None of us can let that happen. I pull at my four-leaf clover bulleted necklace.

Eddie shouts to Baako. "Keep up, Baako. Where did you learn to ride a horse?"

"Didn't." Baako shifts on his horse trying to hold on and looking like he might fall off any minute.

Eddie stops beside Baako and shoves him into an upright position. "Sit like this and grab his mane." He takes a handful of the horsehair to show Baako.

Baako grips the mane. "Yeah, that does work better."

Eddie, the consummate frontiersman, and Baako, the servant. They couldn't be any more different, but I like the company.

Hershey is my chocolate colored horse. I love her because when we were quarantined on the farm all of those years, I would sneak out and feed her stolen fruit from our harvest. I claimed her as mine even before I made her mine.

Our dilapidated farmhouse, my home, stands tall and proud. A two-room shack with boards clutching strong to the side of the walls. The paint is peeling. Can't remember what color it's supposed to be. The ripped screen holds on by a hinge that hugs one side of the main door. The inside door is warped and barely shuts.

Are the children still using the raggedy sofa? What changes have they made?

Baako and Eddie herd the children out of the barn. I wave. Time enough for pleasantries later.

Before I enter the main house, I'm on a mission to ride my Ferris wheel. Been too long since I've felt the breeze through my hair. My heart flutters in anticipation as I slowly make my way to the metal giant, memorizing every step to recall later.

Scary to think about what the world will be like if we allow the Mercs to take over. Right now slaves are leaving their owners. The rich are having a hard time fending for themselves. They don't know how to take care of their own needs. Always had someone doing for them. It's a change they are not equipped to handle.

The privileged desperately want to purchase a guarantee to be virus free. But they don't have the cure. We do. The virus remedy administered to me and being distributed to the rest of the resistance is a major comfort.

The Mercs will eventually hear about our vaccine. I worry about my half-siblings, the princess, the new prince, and the queen. Soon, I'll have to go and save them. But for now, I'll ride my Ferris wheel and celebrate love as I think about the wedding between my sister, Gretel, and my best friend, Colt.

The Ferris wheel has been on our farm as long as I can remember. I love it, even though it's rusty, tattered, and the color of a rotten banana peel. I slump into the bottom chair, causing it to sway. I hit the "on" lever and it ascends with creaking movements.

As I fall back in the corroded passenger car, it rocks back and forth like the pendulum on the black forest cuckoo clock that keeps time in our living room. The night fills with rusty scraping sounds; then after a moment or two, nothing but serene silence is left.

Riding the Ferris wheel allows me to look out over the farm. The harvests have been neglected. It will take time to bring these crops back to life. Maybe Riley would like to try farm life again after this is all over. A warm sensation tingles my senses.

From my Ferris wheel perch, I take in hints of grass peeking out of the shimmering snow and watch the hills roll into the evening darkness.

A disturbing scene unfolds as I watch from the top of the wheel. From out of nowhere, four men ride horses onto the farm. Who are they? Mercs? Why are Mercs here? They are supposed to be in hiding, fearful of the virus's return. Something's wrong.

The men approach Eddie and Baako and huddle them and the children together. A surprise attack? Hurriedly one of the men, Eddie, Baako, and the children disappear into the forest's edge. Why are they leaving?

Nothing to do, but watch from my spot in the clouds. My heart sinks. Fearing the worst, I listen for gunshots. No shots. No screams. No sounds. What's going on?

The other three men scan the area. One man goes to the farmhouse door and unbolts it. It swings open. One of the men spies me on the Ferris wheel. He points.

They're looking for me. The three of them head over to the wheel. Are they going to kill me now? After all of this, why now?

I grasp the four-leaf clover one last time as I come to the bottom of the Ferris wheel. I reach over and pull the lever to stop it. I step out ready to take my punishment.

Let them come to me. I take a deep breath and wait, readying myself.

The curve of one man's face is familiar to me. So is his gait. Do I know this Merc? I hope not. Mercs are merciless. They kill and ask questions later. I take a deep breath. The man turns and faces me.

How can this be and what does this mean?

It's my father—the ambassador. How can he be alive? Everyone thought he was dead. He was supposed to have died in a car explosion.

One of the other men grabs my arm as I stand on the concrete at the bottom of the wheel. Like a crack of lightning, a loud sound sends a shock through me before I see blood spray on the bottom chair of the Ferris wheel. The man's hand drops from my arm and he falls forward. The force of his head hitting the concrete below the Ferris wheel makes a horrible thudding noise. The sight of the syrupy red puddle turns my stomach.

I gag as the other man lifts me off my feet and runs in a zigzag line behind my father towards the open door of our farmhouse. As my father clears the outside door, another shot rings out. I glance to the side and see a hole in the wall of the house. Only a few inches away from my face. A bullet.

The other man sets me on the floor. No time to wonder about why my father who I thought had perished in a car explosion is now standing beside me out of breath. He yells orders to the other man. "We have to get out of here or we'll all be killed."

My mind immediately visualizes the children. They'll be slaughtered. They have been here for months training for battle. This farm is supposed to be one of the safest place on earth. Why are these people shooting at us? We've been so careful.

"Are they coming for you?" I glare at my father. "Who's shooting at us?"

"Mercs." My father counts the square pieces in the floor. "One, two, three...here. It's under here." He grabs the corner of the huge ornate table that sits in front of the dilapidated sofa. He is careful not to scratch the floor. It's heavy and he struggles to lift it.

The other man yanks at one side and it finally moves. The two of them heave the table, exposing a piece of the plywood floor. The piece has a hole on one side. The other man holds up the table. Blood covers his shirt. Is he hurt?

My father puts his fingers in the hole and lifts the corner of the plywood. As he pulls it up, I peer into the void below. Dark, no source of light. It's a trap door. I've lived here all of my life. I never knew about that trap door.

"What about the children and where are Baako and Eddie?" I can't forget about them. We were supposed to gather the children and go back to Aunt Sandra's compound. Now I don't know where they are and I'm in the middle of gunfire.

The two men ignore my pleas, motioning for me to be quiet. My father slides through the trap door under the floor and disappears into the darkness.

He pulls at my feet and I struggle against him. "I can't just leave the others!"

Another bullet pierces the door and hits the sofa right beside where I am standing. Feathers fly.

"Not now." My father tugs hard at my ankle. "Push her." The other man shoves me from behind into the hole in the floor. I'm no match for the two of them. Off balance, I topple into the void. My father cushions my fall as I knock hard into the dirt sides of the opening. I swallow dirt and cough.

The two men work quickly to pull the heavy table over their heads and center it back over the plywood piece disguised as a part of the floor. They snap the plywood back over the opening of the trap door until it drops into place above us just as we hear footsteps.

"Who..." Dirt sprinkles in my face.

My father clamps his hand over my mouth and whispers in my ear. "Guns."

It's dark and I can't see the muddy soil, but I feel it. I know the gun men are walking on the rug above. The sounds of their footsteps echo in the chamber below. We have escaped certain death by seconds.

Muffled voices sound in the living room, soft at first and then loud. No way to know how many. I can't make out what they are saying, but they sound angry. It's dark in the cave area. I touch the sides. More dirt. I reach out my hand and swipe at nothingness. It's void both ways. Hollow. An underground tunnel to where?

It's dark and I try to stand. The tunnel is not high enough to accommodate our height. I get down on all fours. I know my father is crouching also. He reaches back and grabs a wad of my hair before finding my shoulder and pulling me forward behind him.

The other man shoves me from behind. I reach around to feel behind me and touch the man covered in a warm sticky substance. I hope it is not blood. But if it is, I hope that it's not his. I'm wedged in between them. I have no choice but to follow.

My head slams into a hanging part of the cave, which causes a chunk of dirt to fall in my way. I crawl over the mass, smashing it with my knee as I pass, knocking into the sides more than once.

The tunnel is rough and attempting to avoid the protrusions jutting down from the top, sides, and bottom proves difficult. Impossible with the sight factor down to nil. I slam once again into the side of the cave and dirt flies, as we three hurry to make the distance between the trapdoor and wherever we are heading.

The man behind me is moving quickly. Maybe he isn't hurt and the blood on his shirt isn't his. I hope so anyway. I struggle to block all thoughts of the children, Baako, and Eddie and what might be happening to them. I can't think about that right now.

It seems like a long time before we come to a stop. My father opens another plywood door above him. This floor is covered by a rug, which he quickly throws off to the side. A light ray falls into the tunnel. It's my first look at our passage. Exactly what I thought. A crudely dug tunnel. No idea how long it has been here. Could be since the first or second world war for all I know.

My father lifts himself out and then pulls me through. He grips my arms and jerks me up almost wrenching my shoulder out of joint. The other man has a hand on my derrière and shoves me the last bit out of the hole. After he quickly pulls himself up, they replace the door and cover it with the rug.

We are in another farmhouse I don't recognize. It is similar to mine. A threadbare, raggedy sofa sits in the living room. How many of these escape tunnels are there?

An intricate path of trap doors, an underground tunnel escape route between houses. For the twelve years of quarantine, I never knew. This knowledge could have changed everything back then. Why would anyone keep this a secret? It takes a moment, but I process why. We were in quarantine. If we had travelled through the tunnels, the virus could have spread. It was probably safer that we didn't know. I would not have been able to resist the idea of seeing others. I know I would have used the tunnels.

No words have been spoken since we got into the tunnel. Quiet is better right now since all my questions would be about what is happening to the children and the others and I'm not sure I could handle the answer at this moment.

My father opens the outside door of the farmhouse slightly and then motions for the man and me to follow him out. We run through the woods for a long while before we stop. My father removes some brush that turns out to be covering a cave door. This is a cave I know. It's where we keep supplies for Undesirables and Uncounteds to hide out.

As we enter, my father picks up matches by the door, easily lights a kerosene lantern located at the entrance and illuminates the contents of our haven. Huge water jugs rest on the floor. It the first time I've taken a full breath since my ride on the Ferris wheel.

The reality hits me. The children are probably slaughtered. Baako and Eddie are most likely dead. I cradle my head with my arms and sob, loud and sloppy. I can't stop. All of these people are dead and I did nothing to stop it. What kind of monster does that make me?

Chapter 2

"We have to go back!" Each of my words is accentuated by spewing snot and spit.

My father grabs my shoulders and shoves me down on a box.

I lean my head back on the gritty dirt wall. "We can't just leave them there. They don't know about the tunnel. How can they escape?"

"I'm not sure that they can, but we can't go back." My father's face is ashen. "I'm sorry." He turns his attention to the other man. I notice him now. It's the first time I've looked at him since the Ferris wheel. He's covered in blood.

My father asks, "Were you hit?"

The man mumbles and grits his teeth. "Yeah, that last bullet got me in the shoulder." After the man sits, he pulls his shirt off, exposing a large gash. I retch as I look at the blood spurting out of it. It shows no signs of stopping. I'm no doctor, but it looks bad.

My father squats beside him. "Charles, I don't know how you made it this far with this gunshot wound."

"That's what bodyguards do." The man who in essence saved my life a few minutes ago is stretched out on the cavern floor bleeding to death.

Searching around our safe house, I find a rag and stuff it in the wound in an attempt to stop the gushing blood. "We have to help him."

Charles grips my hand, which is still holding the bloody rag. "I appreciate it, but I'm afraid that I'm done for. I knew the risks and I've seen enough wounds to know that I've been hit in a vital place. The blood loss cannot be overcome."

Tears stream down my face. "There has to be something we can do."

Charles reaches for my face and wipes away a tear. "Paisley, I'm glad I got to meet you. I listen to your and Colt's broadcast. It has given me and scores of others hope. You are the face of freedom and I am honored to have helped you escape."

I turn to my father who is sitting silently with a solemn look on his face. I ask, "What does he mean? Wasn't he here to guard you?"

My father doesn't have a chance to answer before Charles emits a low groan. His back arches for a moment before all of the breath in his lungs exhales. He dies staring into my eyes and gripping my hand. As his grip loosens, the life in his eyes evaporates and all that is left is a blank stare. I carefully run my hand over his eyes to close them. Now he looks as if he is sleeping. It gives me comfort. Maybe I want to block out the ugliness. I don't know.

I sit quietly with him for a few moments. His was a quiet death. The look on his face is peaceful. It takes a minute for me to process before my heart breaks. I didn't even know him, but he gave his life to save me.

That is what we Uncounteds and Undesirables do. We sacrifice. My blood boils as I think of the pampered royals and their carefree, sheltered life. Is this what we have to look forward to in this battle for democracy?

We sit silently for a few more minutes. My father finally rises, finds a large piece of fabric, and covers Charles. He takes twine, wraps it around Charles's body, and ties the rags around his feet and at his head. "We will carry him out and try to give him a proper burial when things calm down."

"How many more will we have to bury?" I cover my face with my hands.

My father doesn't answer, but his defeated look gives me all the information I need. It's going to be bad. Faces of the dear children flash in my mind and I take in a deep breath. We have no weapons in here. If the Mercs are storming the farm, we have no chance to fight them off.

"We can't save the children, can we?"

He doesn't answer again, quietly patting Charles as a tear runs down his face. The realization that the smartest move is to stay here and not go back and help the others makes me choke. I succumb to the gagging reflex and vomit in the corner. It takes me a few minutes to recover.

"You okay?" My father asks.

Dipping my head slightly, it's my turn not to answer. My stomach is empty, but the smell of the puke is overwhelming in such close quarters. I have to try to make this right. It's enough to be trapped in a cave with a dead friend. Vomit in the corner is just one too many smells to deal with.

Spying a half-eaten jar of pears, I open it and use another rag to scrape the vomit clinging to the dirt floor into the jar. I choke some more as I am doing this. Fortunately, with an empty stomach, it's just dry heaves. It takes me a while to get the vomit into the jar, between scraping and then heaving when the smell gets the better of me. I finally get all of the vomit and surrounding dirt sealed up. I can only hope that time will mask the smell.

My father takes out a piece of fruit from a fresh jar and waves it around the cavern. "This might help too."

In a few moments, sereneness takes over and I settle. I can't help the children, all I can do is hope that they survive. It's going to be a long night.

Not sure how long we sit there. Finally, my voice pierces the silence. "What did Charles mean he was here to protect me? I thought he came with you." I stop and glare at my father. "What's going on?"

"You need an explanation." My father has no sense of urgency at all in his voice. How could he be some calm? People are dead.

I turn to face him. "An explanation. Yes, an explanation would be nice. While you are at it, how about explain just how are you alive? Everyone was told you were dead."

He lets out a deep breath. "I faked my own death."

"Faked your death?" I clomp around the cave waving my arms. "What about your family? You had just found out that I, your long lost daughter, was still

19

alive. For goodness sakes, your wife was pregnant. You left her and the princess with no protection."

I point my finger at him. "The queen has been suffering a deep depression. Not a good thing for a pregnant woman. The queen really loves you. She's been inconsolable." I glare at him. "Did you even know that the baby was born? How could you leave them?"

The expression on his face gives away his emotions. Guilt. Sadness. Almost to the point of defeat. "I know my son was born." His face contorts again and the tortured look is replaced by a look of anger. He growls. "I also know that she has married the evil Emperor Richard."

His voice is so full of pain. I reach out and grab his hand, but he pulls away. I can't help, but feel sorry for him. I say, "We won't stand for the manipulation and everything it means for the poor. If it's any consolation, I think the queen was pushed into marrying Emperor Richard. We have been trying to organize a revolt of the Undesirables and Uncounteds. The poor."

He takes in a deep breath and as he releases it, his look softens. "I have to control myself if we have any hope of overthrowing the emperor's evil regime." The edges of his mouth turn up slightly. "I've been following your rogue radio broadcasts." He squeezes my hand. "You've made me so proud."

My chest puffs. "I haven't done it alone. You know that Oliver is with us." Oliver, my long lost brother.

He takes in a labored breath. "Did you tell him you are his sister?"

"How could I?" I cross my arms. "What kind of explanation would that have been? Hi, Oliver. It seems that before the virus happened to the world, me, you, our father, and our mother were living on a military base in Germany." I uncross my arms. "After the virus outbreak, you and father escaped to America, leaving my mother to perish, and me to be adopted by a German family who raised me as their own. Yeah, that's what happened. What do you think he would have said?"

Father nodded. "He'd have thought you were crazy. Not telling him was a better choice."

"Thanks." I didn't really know what to call my father. I didn't feel comfortable calling him dad since I didn't really know him. The man who raised me, my real father, had died long ago. It seemed disrespectful to him to call the ambassador "dad."

I cut my eyes over at my father. He wasn't the only one keeping secrets. I certainly couldn't tell him my suspicion that our mother hadn't actually died, but is alive and a leading force in the rebellion. I think his wife being married to the brutal dictator and his new baby and little girl being raised by him might be all the news he could handle right now.

Changing the subject seems like the best course of action. "Why did you come to the farm?"

"We came to save you. We heard that the Mercs were planning to raid on this farm as soon as you or Colt showed up. Our sources alerted us to the fact that you were indeed travelling here. I'm glad we made it to you in time."

"What about the others with you?"

"It's not what you think." He pulls out a jar of pears and opens it. He hands it to me.

I shake my head. "Just puked, remember? Think I should wait a while before eating."

He eats the pear himself and moves the jar away from me. "Probably a good idea."

There is something I'm desperate to know. "Do you know anything about the children and Eddie and Baako?"

"They should be fine. One of our group took them away before the gunfire started. Charles and I weren't alone. But you need to stay hidden for a while." He sits beside me, grabs out a pear, and swallows it whole.

"Why did they attack the farm?" It makes no sense to me. "The children have been safe for months now with no sign of trouble. Why now?"

"The king is dead."

He says it so matter of factly that I lose my breath. The king. I hated the king. He controlled distribution of the root that helps cure the virus. I'd personally witnessed him killing Undesirables, those in our world who are not perfect because of disability or disfigurement, and the Uncounteds, those in our world who have no family and are alone. He was evil. He preyed on those weaker than him. I hate to admit it, but this news makes me happy. I'm happy that the king is dead. "Why is that a bad thing?" I surprise myself with my calmness in speaking of another's demise.

"The evil Emperor Richard is now in control."

Chapter 3

A day passes. I wake to see a dark silhouette hovering over me. The stranger leans down and shakes my father awake. "Ambassador Grayson."

"Yes, I'm here." My father bolts upright, rubbing the sleep out of his eyes. "Hello, Soldier. Glad to see you. Is it safe?"

The soldier shifts his rifle to his shoulder and pulls my father to his feet. "As safe as it's going to be for a while. We need to get you back to base camp."

My father pulls my arm helping me to my feet. "We have to get Paisley to safety first. She is the top priority now."

The soldier dips his head. "Paisley. What an honor." He salutes me.

I raise my hand quickly to my forehead trying to copy his salute. It seems like the right thing to do. "What about the farm children, Baako and Eddie? Did they survive?"

His head drops. "Not sure. We lost a few, but most survived. We did take out that Merc patrol." He pauses.

My father looks at him. "But..."

"We wanted to have you hide here longer, but unfortunately one of the Merc patrol got away. We are afraid he'll report to the others. That's why I am here. It's imperative that we move from this area. It will be crawling with Mercs soon." He looks around. "Where are Charles and Roger?"

My father pats the soldier's shoulder. "Roger died at the farm and..." He points to the canvas. "Charles didn't make it either. We need to bury him."

The soldier's face drops and he turns ashen. "No time."

I step in front of my father. "We can't just leave him here."

The soldier locks his eyes with mine and says, "You're right, I'll carry him. We will bury him when we are safe."

My breath calms and I feel my features soften. "Thanks. What's your name?"

"Donald."

Donald pulls a handgun out of his pocket, gives it to my father, and wastes no time heaving the canvas-covered body over his shoulder. He crouches through the cave door. It's completely dark. He says, "We'll travel at night. It's safer."

I'm glad that Donald is with us because with no source of light we are completely vulnerable to the treacherous hills and cliffs that make up the terrain of this part of Bavaria. He tethers the three of us together and we travel single file. Donald leads, carrying the body, I follow, and my father is behind me. It's unbelievable how far we travel in a short time. We have no chance to slow down with us tied to Donald and following his track speed. It helps that we have no fear of slipping or falling.

Donald stops all at once. "There are signs of Mercs closing in on this area. We need to hurry." He motions to the side. "Be careful. There is a deep ravine over to the left side. Make sure you match my steps. One fall and you're a goner." How he can see this with the darkness is beyond me, but I don't question.

My father asks, "How can we go faster?"

Donald heaves Charles's body down into the ravine. "I know it was a terrible thing to do, but this is the ravine that many bodies are thrown over. It won't be noticed. I'm sorry Paisley. I know you wanted to bury him proper."

A tear escapes my eye and runs down my cheek. "I did, but I believe that Charles would want us to survive." I peer towards the ravine and whisper. "Thank you my sweet Charles for giving your life for me. I won't let your sacrifice be in vain. I will do everything in my power to survive and complete the mission."

Without the added weight, we triple our moving time. I am unable to keep with the gait of the long legged men and Donald finally untethers me and squats down. "On my back," he orders.

I obey. I can't argue. I know I can't keep up. I am jostled as he runs full speed. Jumping over crevasses and climbing hills like a monkey scaling a tree. I hear my father struggling to keep up. His breathing is hard and labored, but he does not complain.

As the sun rises, we arrive at familiar place. It's the entrance to Aunt Sandra's lands. I recognize the bushes and see the back of the cart. It's a proven safe haven. Aunt Sandra has managed to keep the whereabouts secret for years.

"There's our girl." It's Aunt Sandra. Her gray hair flies in every direction and her smile reassures me. She uses her cane to step out of her carriage. "I thought you might like to see a familiar face." I throw myself off the back of Donald and run toward her, encircling her in a big bear hug.

Colt and my sister, Gretel, who were married a few nights ago, appear from behind the bush. My heart dances and I feel a sense of calmness. I'm with my family.

My father bows slightly to Aunt Sandra. "Donald and I are going back to Hamburg. We are needed there."

Aunt Sandra squeezes my father's hand. "Thanks so much for finding Paisley and bringing her back to us. She doesn't realize how important she is to the resistance."

My father smiles at me. "She's important to me too." He winks at me. "More than you know." He hugs my shoulder. "I'm sorry that I can't stay here with you, but I must help my son, Oliver. He is doing dangerous work. Drake has gathered the resistance fighters from around the world. Together they are making up a plan. Lieutenant Drake and an American woman leader, Captain Via."

Captain Via, I met her when I escaped from America. Through talking to Oliver, my brother who doesn't know he's my brother, I have a sneaking suspicion that Captain Via may be mine and Oliver's mother and the ambassador's long lost wife. Of course,

I can't tell my father of this because I don't know it for sure. Plus, he's already married the queen. Wait! The queen is now married to Emperor Richard. What a mess! Maybe after this war we can straighten all of this up. I smile a little inside. It's my only salvation; I must find humor in the craziness of it all.

Enough of that mixed-up thinking. I certainly can't fix it all. I direct my attention to my sister, Gretel, and Colt, her new husband (and my best friend). I squeeze them both hard. "Sorry about interrupting the honeymoon." Tears that I can't control run down my face.

Gretel brushes my hair. "It's fine. There is plenty of time for a proper honeymoon after all of this is over. We were so worried when we heard about the king."

Pausing for a moment, I ask, "Does anyone know how he actually died? It seems awfully convenient for the Emperor. He just married the queen and her father, the king and ruler of all, dies."

My father nods. "That is why it is imperative that we get back to Hamburg at once. We must sort out all of this and try to control the misinformation being disseminated daily by the evil emperor. We thought the king was evil. The king is nothing compared to this maniac."

Aunt Sandra extends her hand. "Please sir, let me thank you once again."

My father shakes her hand. "Of course."

She squeezes his elbow with her other hand. "I don't think you realize how important it was that you sent your men to save the children on Paisley's farm. If those children had died..." her voice trails off.

"But they didn't, Aunt Sandra." Gretel smiles at her. "They're safe."

Aunt Sandra points to the hidden corral of horses. "Even your horse, Hershey, made it back. My boys found the group from your farm hiding back a ways and brought them here."

"The children are alive!" My hearts jumps for joy. I walk over and pet Hershey. "I love you, my sweet horsie."

My father turns to me. "You are in good hands now. I will take my leave. I am sure that you and I will run into each other again. When this is all over..."

Deep in my heart, I know what he wants to say. When this is over, we will pick up the pieces of our lives and sort through all of this. But him being my father is still a secret so I simply say, "I know."

Aunt Sandra motions to the horse. "Please ambassador, take two of the horses. It will make your ride a lot easier."

My father nods. "Thank you." He smiles at me. "Don't worry. We won't take your favorite." He and Donald pick two of the horses, leaving Hershey behind.

It's difficult watching my father ride off, but I know that my brother could use his help and I definitely know that the resistance needs him. The Consortium of the World will be convening in a few months to vote on how our world will be run. We want a democracy and the royals and Mercs want a dictatorship. Our side must win.

After my father rides off, I stare at Colt. "I'm so glad the children are safe. What about Eddie and Baako?"

"They're fine." Gretel guides me to the wagon. "One casualty. A child."

It's hard for me to hold back my sorrow. A child who would never see the teenage years. I spit out the words rolling in my head. "What kind of war would prey on innocent children? What kind of monster would order their murder?"

Colt lifts me into the wagon. "An unjust war that we are going to stop. Are we ready to end this thing?"

I stand defiantly and look around. "More than ever. Do we have a plan?"

"Yes." Colt's face is stern and full of hate. "Kill Emperor Richard.

Chapter 4

Aunt Sandra bounces down the uneven trail in her horse drawn wagon coach as the rest of us trail behind her in the dense wooded area. We tramp deep into the forest until we come upon a vineyard with vines so thick they are almost impassable. The horses are skittish, but allow themselves to be led. At the clearing stands a large concrete barrier fence covered completely with greenery.

"You count it off, Paisley." Aunt Sandra says.

I number the bricks on the wall, one hundred and thirty four, before stopping. Reaching into the mass of vines, I unlock the gate. We carefully conceal Aunt Sandra's buggy and corral the horses in a hidden area before we make our way down the path through the cave. At the threshold, we come upon two sentries guarding the entrance. They bow when they spy Aunt

Sandra. About a kilometer ahead beyond the maze, the tops of the tower spikes peek through.

I'm tired and out of breath, but the sight makes me smile. "We're here."

"Almost, dear." Aunt Sandra points to the towers. "You know they're not as close as you think." She winks at me.

Aunt Sandra motions to a few of the boys who have run to greet us and says, "The boys will lead you through the maze." Along the way, I bump into the sides and stumble on the uneven terrain. It's not like when I went through the maze the first time blindfolded. I thought the maze was made out of bristled vines. But it's not, it's a thick hedge.

The hedge grows in so many different ways that it causes prickly points and unevenness. It'd be nice if it were trimmed in a perfect square. But that won't happen anytime soon. We go forward then backwards, and then wade through a stream.

The climb up the ladder is last. Aunt Sandra is carried by one or two boys at all times. Finally, in front of us stands Aunt Sandra's castle. The structure's regal splendor begs respect. I am so happy to be back that I give the magnificent place a little royal-like curtsy.

We follow Aunt Sandra across the open drawbridge of the dried up moat. The inside assembly houses a massive courtyard which is visible when Aunt Sandra opens the outside gate allowing us to pass into the main quarters.

"Paisley!" Riley throws himself onto me with such force that I teeter. "They wouldn't allow me to come."

"Let her breathe." Gretel pulls him off me. "You're going to choke her. Remember, she was almost killed. Give her some room."

Gretel, Colt, Riley, and I make our way to the large dining room table.

"What happened?" Gretel asks.

Slumping in the chair, it's the first time I feel really safe. "We had just gotten to the farm when they started shooting at us. Have you seen Baako and Eddie?"

Gretel shakes her head and motions to Colt to bring a jug of water. She pours me a glass. "Drink some."

"Not thirsty." I push the water away. "I thought that the Mercs believed the virus was back. If that's true, why did they attack us?"

"That's right. You don't know what happened." Riley brushes his hair out of his face and slaps dirt off his knee with his hand. "Some of Emperor Richard's men intercepted a message being sent to the Americas exposing our ruse. They realized that we had been lying all the time and decided to orchestrate a surprise attack and it almost succeeded."

 I throw my hands up in disbelief. "How did *we* find out about it?"

Riley explains, "One of the children overheard them planning the strike. Unfortunately, she was captured soon after that. The Mercs thought they had killed her and threw her down a ravine. She managed to crawl out and we found her. She was barely alive. Before she died, she told us about their plans. She gave her life to get that information to us."

Tears well in my eyes, "Who?"

Gretel whispers, "Kelley."

Kelley, the child who had led us to Aunt Sandra's in the first place, was a hero. My mind flashed to an image of Kelley playing with the other children in the courtyard. So innocent, so full of excitement with so much of her life in front of her. Not fair. Not fair at all. My face reddens and I pound my fist in the air. "How can we ask these young children to fight this war?"

Gretel cradles me in her arms. "How can we not?"

Gretel is right. In order to be victorious, we have to enlist everyone available. The Mercs are a formidable foe. Not to be taken lightly. We have to win. No matter the cost. My stomach churns. I vomit for the second time in two days.

"That's enough for today." Gretel rubs my hair. "You need to sleep."

"What about this mess?" I point to the fresh throw up. An older woman comes in with a mop and it is clean almost before I get my question out.

"Time for your own bed." Riley stands up and pulls me to my feet. "I'll walk you."

Riley helps me back to my quarters. He stands at the door and points to my bed. "Get some rest. We can figure this out tomorrow. Today you should take it easy."

Reaching for the four-leaf clover bulleted necklace, I begin to twirl it in my fingers. "This thing always saves me. Every time I think that I'm about to die, it pulls me through. It is such a powerful good luck charm. I *should* give it back to you."

Riley clasps his hands around mine. "No, keep it. If it keeps you safe, it's doing its job. I don't know what I'd do without you. When I heard that your farm had been attacked, I died a little inside. You don't know how much you mean to me." He brushes my hair back with his hand. I like his touch. I like it more than I should.

"You made it!" Eddie rushes through the door knocking Riley away and wraps his arms around me. "I can't believe you survived all those bullets."

36

"Eddie's right." Baako trots in after him. "It's a miracle you're alive. I thought for sure you were dead."

Baako throws his arms around me and Eddie. "And the ambassador is alive too." I teeter backward from the force of the hugs.

Riley jerks Baako and Eddie away and uprights me. "She's been through enough today. She needs to rest." Riley pushes me through the door and shuts it behind me.

Their voices fade from the door as I plop down on the bed. Riley is right. It's been a long day. I don't realize how tired I am until my head rests on the pillow. My eyes slam shut.

No idea how long I sleep. When I finally come out of the room, the compound is bustling with activity. People are scurrying about carrying supplies and in the courtyard, buggies are being loaded. I see Baako and ask, "What's going on?"

"War." Baako whispers.

Chapter 5

"**W**ar?"

"Yes." Baako stops moving for a minute. "Haven't you heard? We just got word that Emperor Richard is telling everyone that we, the resistance, released the virus back into the population on purpose and that we hold a virus inoculation, but we're refusing to give it to anyone." He shifts a large load of wood from one shoulder to the other. He struggles to keep it balanced. "I have to go."

"Wait." I grab his shirtsleeve. "Where's Riley?"

"He left for Hamburg this morning." Baako scurries off, juggling his heavy load.

Riley's gone? Why would Riley leave without telling me? Wait, I'm not the boss of him! Of course, Riley has every right to do whatever he wants. What if I wanted to leave? Would I go and report to Riley? Of course not. I shake my head. Don't think about Riley. Focus!

I have to find Colt, Gretel, or Aunt Sandra. I can't believe I slept so long. Was war declared while I was dreaming?

Everyone must be at central compound. It's a house in the middle of the compound that is used to discuss strategy and give assignments. I enter the sparse room populated with a couple of tables, a few chairs, books, folders, maps, weapons, and various other war paraphernalia. I'm right. Most of the organizers are here and deep in discussion. Colt hovers over a table full of papers with Eddie.

"Colt, what's going on and why did Riley leave?"

Colt motions for me to take a seat beside him. "We need to catch you up. We have to go on the air tonight. This thing has escalated out of control. I don't know if you heard, but the emperor is blaming the resurgence or fake resurgence of the virus on the resistance. We have to get in front of this misinformation."

Pulling out a stool, I pick up a paper to study. "How did we find out about all of this?"

"Oliver." Gretel announces from the back of the room. "Oliver hacked into their transmissions and found out that *they* have a plan to reintroduce the virus back into the poor communities."

Dropping the paper to the table, I slump in my chair. "What do you mean reintroduce *the virus*? The deadly virus? The one that caused a forced 12-year quarantine? That virus?"

Gretel nods her head as she takes a seat. "Yes, the emperor is not only evil and cruel. He's obviously a madman."

"What is the rationale?" I ask. "It could kill him too."

Colt folds up a paper. "That's the horrible part. He knows we have the cure and that we are inoculating people. He is trying to force us to reveal the formula."

"Shouldn't we?" I ask.

Gretel pats my hand. "Of course everyone should have the inoculation, but we can't let him control it. Then it will not get to everyone. It will be saved just for the rich."

"No way!" I shake my head. "Can't we give him the formula and still control our part?"

Gretel takes a deep breath. "What a nice thought. Unfortunately, you need trained scientists to make the formula." Her eyes widen. "We can't give him any of our scientists."

"Do we know how far the emperor is willing to go?"

Colt stands up. "That's the bad part. From our sources, his plan is to inject people with the virus until we surface. Once he gets the inoculations, he will control the world's health. From what I hear, once he is able to make the formula, he will wipe us out so we can't give the cure for free. We can't let that happen."

"Even if..." Can I really ask the question, if I don't want to hear the answer?

Gretel answers, "Even if people die." She swallows hard. "Paisley, you know I'm a nurse for all practical purposes. If you would have told me a year ago I would let anyone die if I had the means to save them, I would have told you that you were crazy, but now..."

"It's not right." I can't believe this. My sister is willing to let innocents die. "Let's give them the cure. We'll keep some for ourselves."

Colt pipes up. "No, not a chance."

I turn to Colt. "Why not?"

"We have to give up something irreplaceable. Because the only way that can happen is if Gretel takes the inoculation to them and shows them how to manufacture it. I'm not going to let her go."

"No one else can go?" I ask.

"One other person could." Gretel answers, "But we are *certainly* not going to let him go there."

"Who?" I ask.

"The ambassador." Colt answers.

There are only two people in the world who can synthesize the inoculations. One is supposed to be dead and the other is my sister. I understand now.

"Show me how to synthesize it." I demand. "I'm smart. I could learn how to do it." I stare at Gretel. "Why are you being so secretive? Why can't everyone learn how to do it?"

"Because." Gretel crosses her arms and grunts. "Why do you have to be so hard-headed, Paisley?"

I lean close to my sister's face, nose to nose. I know she can't stand it when I do this. "I want to know why others can't learn how to make the inoculation. Wouldn't that solve the problem?" I wag my finger in her face. "Then it wouldn't be just you and you wouldn't be in so much danger."

"Whoa!" Colt slams his fist on the table. "Then you would put yourself in danger. You and I are the face of the resistance. We have to stay here and let the people know what is going on. Gretel has to be here to synthesize the inoculation."

"Why is the technique such a secret?" I put up my hand. "I understand about Gretel, but why can't others learn?"

Colt's voice rises. "Gretel is not the only irreplaceable part of this. We only have one machine that synthesizes and replicates the cure. The DNA replicator."

Gretel talks over Colt. "We can't give that to the emperor and without it, l can't show them how to make the cure. If the replicator breaks, I don't know how to repair it. Only the ambassador knows how to fix it and he is not here. So if we want to make sure that we keep manufacturing the vaccine, which we *have* to do, I'm the only one who works the machine." She glares at me.

"Do you think I would tear up such an important piece of equipment?" I get close to her again nose-to-nose, breathing onto her face, just like when we were little.

Colt breaks in. "Sisters, quit bickering. It's perfectly reasonable. Gretel doesn't trust anyone else with the machine. So Gretel and only Gretel will synthesize the cure. We will load her lab with people who can measure or bring her things. But she is the only one handling the one of a kind device." He points at Gretel and me. "You two understand?"

We nod and he turns his attention to the others in the room. "Baako and Eddie will organize a group to deliver the inoculations to our resistance group. We all know where the emperor will introduce the virus. It won't be with his rich royal friends. It will be with the poorest of the poor."

Baako looks at me. "It will be the Undesirables and the Uncounteds. It will be those he considers throw-aways."

Gretel chimes in. "It will also be with the people who are owned. The human trafficking problem is out of control. The royals and rich will use their owned people as guinea pigs. It'll be pandemonium. We have no choice. We have to take care of ours first."

It made sense. It just hurt hearing it. Our world had lost so many. We couldn't afford to lose more. "Have we inoculated all of the people on Aunt Sandra's farm?"

Gretel smiles. "Just about. You can make sure that we have. Why don't you take this list around and see that everyone has been up to the medical center and been given the vial of the cure. When you finish you can help me get stuff in the lab while I synthesize the inoculations. The more hands we have in the lab the quicker we can make the antidote."

For the next two hours, I scour the camp looking for anyone who has not been given the vaccine. I don't find a single person. First good news today.

Entering the lab, I don't see Gretel. She must be on break. I look at the vials filled with hope. Such a simple remedy. Just a swallow and you can't contract the virus ever.

Uneasy questions enter my mind. Have my half-sister, the princess, or my half-brother, the prince been inoculated? Does the emperor have access to any of the antidote at all?

I stuff two vials in my pockets. Wouldn't hurt to have two extras for the princess and the prince? I can't help what I'm thinking even though I know how dangerous it will be. Do I have a death wish? It's not in me to stand idly by while my sister and brother die.

Walking out of the lab, I have a specific purpose in mind. My plan is to sneak off Aunt Sandra's land, find the prince and princess, protect them from the illness, and make it back before supper without being caught.

Sounded possible until I listed all of the steps. Oh well, better get started.

Chapter 6

"Paisley? Where do you think you are going?" Colt catches me by the arm. "I know that determined look on your face. Riley said you would try something."

I jerk my arm from his grip. "What does Riley know about what I will or won't do? I'm just checking on the people to make sure they've all been inoculated."

He reaches his hand in my pocket and produces the two vials. "And what are these?"

"Oh those. Extras. Just in case I need to give someone the cure." I mumble unconvincingly.

"Right." Colt turns me around and guides me back into the lab. No use going anywhere or fighting it. There is absolutely no reason to find my brother and sister unless I have the cure in my hand.

Colt walks me to the table. "Sit down." He continues, "Riley begged me and Gretel not to tell you. He was afraid that you would come after him. You won't will you?" He looks deeply into my eyes.

I spring from my seat, but he quickly pushes me back down.

"What does this have to do with Riley?" I jut out my chin and cross my arms. "I don't know what you're talking about. Why would I follow Riley? I don't care what Riley does. Riley means nothing to me at all."

Colt laughs. "Right. But I can tell you mean something to him because he came to us while you were sleeping and asked to do an errand."

My insolent stare chills the room. "What kind of errand?" I pout like a child. "And by the way, what could Riley possibly do that would make a difference to me?"

Colt thumped my forehead with his thumb and finger. "He took the cure to the princess and the new baby. He knew you wouldn't be able to stand it and would insist on taking the cure to them."

My heart flutters. I'm in shock. Riley does know me. "Who went with him?"

"No one. He went by himself. He plans on meeting up with Oliver. It seems that Tury…"

47

"Tury?" I interrupt him. "The lady we found floating in the sea with Baako?" Tury, she was fortunate to be alive. She survived being thrown in the icy ocean with Baako. Certain death. She was lucky to have been found by Colt and me.

Colt continues, "Yeah, Tury. She took your..."

What's he trying to say?

I press him. "She took someone's place?"

"Never mind." He says.

"Where is she? Is she on the ship? How can she get close to the princess and prince?" I drop my head. She's on the ship. I know exactly whose place she is taking. My mother. My mother who was killed by the evil king for the entire world to see on live television. Now the king is dead, but the emperor still lives. A rage boils inside of me. My mother's death sears in my mind. "Tury's working in the kitchen." I whisper.

Colt hugs my shoulder. "She wanted to go to keep an eye on the little prince and princess. She's been reporting to us via Oliver for about a month now. Using Tury to get the cure to the little ones is the perfect plan."

"It is." I have to agree. I rub my temples. Quit obsessing about my mother's murder or Riley being in danger. It's exhausting. "I'm going to go to bed." I trudge to my room and fall onto the mattress.

The next day, I find Gretel in the lab. "Any word on Riley and how he is doing with getting the cure to the children?"

"Nothing yet." Gretel dons her lab coat, picks up a beaker, and swishes the liquids in it. "But we didn't expect it would be quick. I'm sure that Oliver will send word as soon as he knows anything."

"I was just hoping to hear from him." I twirl a test tube in my hand. "What exactly do you want me to do?"

As I fumble the test tube out of my hand and it drops, Gretel catches it. "I really think your expertise would be better used somewhere else."

"Like where?"

"Training the army." She sets the tube in its holder on the counter.

What a great idea! Cooped up in a lab all day is not using my strengths. "Where are they training?"

"Colt has the troops in the southwest quadrant. They start early. The children are out there now. He would love the help." She opens the door for me. "You two finish early to be sure that you make it to the radio broadcast on time tonight. We have to debunk the negative chatter going around about the resistance."

"You're right. One step forward. Five back. It isn't fair. How can the emperor have so much power?"

"We'll figure it out. We have to believe we will win. But we won't be victorious without a trained army." She gives me a quick hug.

"See you later." I take off out the door. It's a beautiful crisp morning. If this place wasn't a training camp for a war and a haven for the persecuted, I could take a few minutes to enjoy it.

Our training area is an open space in the middle of a courtyard. A short stone fence surrounds the space, enclosing it entirely. A gate is used to enter. I imagine centuries ago when this castle was first built on these lands, knights joisted with their swords in the very same pasture. Maybe this exact spot is where the knights learned how to wield their swords and win their battles. I hope some of that good karma is still left on this ground as we train our army of children.

Following a loud voice, I spot Colt yelling at the children. Our trainees are haphazardly milling around as Colt barks orders. "Line up! Let's get together and fall in."

A few of the children hover around Thomas, one of our original army from the Ferris wheel farm. It was his close friend, Kelley who had perished. One girl pats his shoulder. "Sorry. Let me know if you need anything."

Another of our army of children, Amanda hugs a dark haired boy, Parker, and says, "Kelley was such a wonderful person."

"She died helping us all." Parker wipes a tear from his eye. "She was a hero."

"She was wonderful." Thomas chokes back the tears. "I miss her."

Mike sums it all up when he says, "Kelley will always be one of our family. We can't forget her sacrifice and that she died for our freedom.

"Kelley was a wonderful soldier." Colt pulls Thomas in line. "We will all miss her terribly. But we must move on. We must make sure that her death is not in vain."

"Gretel sent me." I walk up and stand by Colt. "She thought my time would be better spent helping you train rather than bothering her in the lab."

His face widens into a grin. "I bet she did. She's particular about her lab. She wants it just so. I think she is worried about that replicator. She is so scared that she is going to tear it up. It's made her question everybody."

"What if Gretel gets sick? Did she ever think about that? She could be sick then none of us would know how to run the machine. What a disaster that could be."

"I'm sure she's thought of that." He shakes his head. "But maybe not. You know I can't talk Gretel out of something once she sets her mind to it. It's like talking to a leaf." He pause for a minute, then he slaps me on the back. "Glad to have you. We make a good team, sister-in-law."

We spend the next few minutes organizing the group.

"Do we get to use weapons?" Mike asks.

Colt drops his arms. "Not yet. But soon."

Mike grins. "I like that."

Parker runs around with his arms formed like a pretend gun. "I'm ready to shoot someone."

Amanda yells at Parker. "Stop, Parker. Be serious. We have to learn the right way to do things or we could get killed."

Wrapping my arm in a stronghold around Parker, I momentarily stop his movements. "Calm down." He jerks away from me, but I grab a hunk of his shirt and refuse to let go. "First, we have to train." Finally, Parker quits squirming, gives up, and sits down to listen.

For the next hour, we put the children through a series of drills. They fight hand-to-hand combat. They crawl on their stomachs practicing evasion maneuvers.

Colt barks, "Perfecting how to elude the enemy is one of the best tactics, we will teach you." He drops down and demonstrates how to hide behind structures. "You need to learn how to sneak up on the opposition and subdue them without calling attention to yourself." He slips up behind Thomas and takes him down by pinning Thomas's arms behind his back and says, "See?"

"Most likely, we will be outgunned and outmanned." I chime in. "The only way we are going to win is for us to be smart. We have a limited supply of guns. We must make weapons out of the terrain, bark, sand, boulders, everything and learn how to use those weapons."

I guide the group over to another section of the training area. On the ground is spread a variety of tree limbs, rocks and other items found in nature. "Here we'll show you how to make dirt bombs, slingshots and catapult throws."

Colt stops me for a minute. "If any of you have an idea of how to make weapons with what we can find out here, please share that information with us. We are going to need all of the help we can get if we have any hope against the emperor's weapons."

"The one thing we have that they don't is a desire to change our way of life." I pick up a rock. "These pampered people have been leading a life of luxury. Although they outnumber us..."

"Why does that matter?" Thomas interrupts. "Aren't the rich lazy? Why are we worried about them fighting?"

"That's a good question, Thomas." I point my finger around the room. "The rich are lazy. That means they aren't going to fight their own battles. Does anyone know who will fight their battles for them?"

Amanda raises her hand and I motion to her. She answers, "They will hire Mercs."

Obviously, Amanda has been paying attention. I nod. "Amanda is right. The rich have no desire to be in the middle of the fray. In fact, they want to stay as far away from it as possible."

I take a breath. "We need to work that to our advantage. Most of the mercenaries are hired. Some of them are like Riley. They are farm boys forced to serve in the mercenary army. I hope that if we win a couple of battles, we can free them. We need to give them a better choice."

A crowd gathers. The children we are supposed to be training make up the front row of our audience. The crowd obscures the stone fence.

Aunt Sandra uses her cane to hobble through the gate and stand beside me. "Don't stop dear. We all need to hear this. You wonder why we want you and Colt to be our voice to the resistance. This is why. While you have been inspiring your young recruits, others have joined them to hear your message too. It's powerful to hear from people who have been in the middle of the battle." Aunt Sandra looks out at the crowd. "Quiet everyone. Let's hear a story to inspire us."

Shrugging my shoulders, I ask Colt. "What should we tell them?"

"I know." Colt begins. "We were just like you. We worked on a farm and did not even know about each other's existence until the Mercs took over our farms and lied to the people. They published falsehoods reporting the Mercs owned the farms. That wasn't true was it?"

The crowd shouts in unison. "NO!"

I say, "Colt and I escaped from our farm with the sole intention of saving my sister and my mother." I feel myself choking up, but hold back the tears. "We searched everywhere and were told that my mother and sister had boarded an ocean liner."

A person in the crowd shouts out. "Your sister is Gretel and you and Colt saved her."

"We wanted to save all of the farm families," Colt says, "I was lucky and found my father and siblings right off. We sent them and the rest of the families to safety to continue our search for Paisley's mother and sister."

Colt paces. "It was then that Paisley and I happened upon Lieutenant Drake. It was the first time we met him. He told us of the underground resistance movement. We knew that if we could get to safety then we would be able to join up with the resistance and here we are."

A shout from the crowd egged us on. "Tell us about the royals."

Another voice asks, "How did you get on that liner?" He looks at the person sitting beside him and whispers, "I love this one. These two are legends."

"One quick story, then we need to get back to work." I continue walking back and forth. Younger children have joined us, some sitting in adult laps. "When we got to Hamburg there was no way to get on the ship. We happened into a doll shop with a kindly owner, Ms. DeVane. We met the princess and her nanny, Miss Brita. Princess Kamea decided that she wanted to add the German dolls to her collection of "Sponsored Companions""

Colt broke in. "And we fit the bill of German dolls. I mean look at me! Don't I look like a living doll?" He puts his hands under his chin, looks up, and smiles. The crowd laughs.

I slap his hands away from his chin. "Ms. DeVane created documents so we could board the ship where we were assigned to play with Princess Kamea. It was fun, but we were owned."

My voice goes solemn. "We are fighting for the Uncounted. The people who are sold to others. We have to stop human trafficking." I look out to the crowd. "How many of you have been owned?" Ninety percent of the hands shoot up.

Colt shouts. "This is unacceptable. How many of you have been deemed Undesirables and slated for annihilation simply because you have a disability or are flawed?"

Many hands shoot up.

"This is not right!" I yell, "Everyone is equal. No person should own other people. Our way of life is broken and we must fix it. We must win this battle. The future is dependent on what we do in the next few months."

I slow my speaking to accentuate every word. I want to be understood. "We have the cure. We control the virus. It can no longer hurt us. The Mercenaries want to take over our world and make it their own.

They want us to serve them. Emperor Richard has stolen the throne and is using it for his own agenda."

Colt trots across the front of the crowd his fist raised, as he yells, "We must win. I say this is our time."

The crowd stands and yells. "YES!"

Colt shouts some more. "They feel the only way to defeat us is from within. They want others to think we are the bad guys."

I shoot my own fist in air. "WE MUST WIN! WE MUST WIN!"

Everyone in the crowd is pumping a fist and chanting. "WE MUST WIN! WE MUST WIN!"

The chant eventually morphs into "WE WILL WIN! WE WILL WIN!"

Aunt Sandra leans in, cups my ear, and whispers, "And that is how you fire up the troops."

I whisper back. "No, that is how you start a war."

Chapter 7

For the next few days, the mood of the compound is one of determination. It sweeps through every nook and cranny of the large area, affecting everyone. Spontaneous chants erupt everywhere. This positive energy makes living on the compound wonderful for these three idyllic days.

Training is great. Everyone is focused. The vaccine is being manufactured by Gretel and her crew in record time. Aunt Sandra and her boys make a plan to deliver the cure to the resistance all over the world.

A large map is set up. Through Oliver, reports of struggles to motivate troops in other places surface. It has proved a more difficult task than first realized. The emperor has massive control over the media and is doing everything he can to undermine the resistance.

There are daily bulletins blaming our side for putting the disease back into the mainstream. They use pictures of dead people, reporting they are casualties of the virus.

Oliver works day and night, releasing stories that contradict this negative influx. He hopes that by reporting the truth to resistance, they will remain loyal to our cause.

Colt and I are summoned to the radio room one morning.

Aunt Sandra stands in front of the massive radio. Wires are hooked at various spots and lights flicker on and off. "It's time for you two to start back on your radio messages." She punches a button on the radio and speaks. "SONOL, they are both here." SONOL is the call sign for Oliver at the resistance's communication center in Hamburg.

The radio squawks and Oliver's voice is heard. "We have some good news for you."

Good news? My heart skips. "What news?"

Oliver's voice sounds again. "Your friend has reported that the cure has been delivered to the two packages. There is no chance they will contract the virus."

Reading between the lines I realize Riley was able to get the cure to the prince and princess. I grab the microphone and press the button. "What about my friend? Is he okay? When is he coming home? Any word on the queen?"

"Be careful about names." Aunt Sandra takes the microphone away from me and presses the button.

Oliver's voice comes back on. "This should be a secure line. But it's always better to be careful."

Aunt Sandra speaks in the speaker. "Don't worry about telling us when our friend will return, dear."

I jerk it back. "Yes, SONOL, worry about it now. I want to know when my friend is coming back."

A familiar voice sounds. "So you miss me."

Riley.

The speaking device drops from my hand and Colt catches it mid-air. "Yeah, we *all* miss you. What happened?"

Riley and Oliver report using a code without people's names and the ship's name about how Riley was able to sneak the cure onto the ship via some supplies that were delivered to the kitchen. Tury intercepted them and followed the directions giving the vials not only the prince and princess, but to the rest of the other "Sponsored Companions" who were still captives.

After they finish, Aunt Sandra asks, "Did the main man make it?"

My father's voice comes on next. "Yes. I'm here and we're working on a plan. As soon as it's finalized, we will get together and implement."

Aunt Sandra cocks her head. "Lieutenant, will the plan work?"

Lieutenant Drake's voice sounds. "I hope so. It's the only chance we have."

For the next hour, Colt and I are instructed by Lieutenant Drake, Oliver, and my father regarding exactly what they want us to say on the address to the troops.

As we are leaving, I ask Colt, "How do you think the young ones are progressing in their training?"

Colt shakes his head. "As well as can be expected. The problem is we are expecting young children, children under fifteen, to be in charge of groups of twenty or so. It will be hard for them to make decisions. They're too young. It's too much responsibility. I wish we had more experienced people to be in charge."

"Funny you should say that." I knock into his shoulder. "Did you forget that I'm sixteen and you are eighteen? How are we any more qualified to lead the entire revolution? I think we have to realize the future we are trying to create is the world people like me and you, the young people, will have to live in. We want to be free. We are the ones who will be living in that new world."

Colt kicks a piece of dirt. "You're right. Some of *us* will be in charge."

"Scary thought, huh?" We both chuckle. I love it when something is funny. There is so little in the world that is humorous nowadays.

Throughout the rest of the day, we work on the script for the presentation we are to report to the troops tonight. Many people labor over every word, making sure that we say everything just right to not give away any information about troops, the resistance in general, or anything about the cure and its location.

It's finally time.

"Paisley and Colt with a message for the resistance troops." Aunt Sandra introduces us.

Colt starts. "Fellow resistance fighters, it has been far too long since Paisley and I have addressed you. I know that you are hearing through the media that the resistance has brought back the virus. That is simply not true. We are here to tell you the truth."

"There was a rumor the virus had started back up." I take a deep breath. "That's not true. We, the resistance fighters, did indeed start that rumor. Our purpose was to try to limit the movements of the mercenaries and royals and those opposing democracy, allowing us to move freely. We had hoped to get information to the troops more easily and try to organize our side."

Colt clears his throat. "Unfortunately, our secret plan was intercepted by Emperor Richard and now is being used to undermine our regime."

"We must not let that happen." I interrupt. "It is imperative that we stay the course."

"There is good news." Colt says. "It could very well be the changing point of the entire war."

"Great news." I am hopeful that all is not lost.

Colt points to the paper. He wants me to follow the script. I hate following orders. Colt continues. "We, the resistance, have indeed found a cure. It was developed by a lab assistant in the ambassador's lab."

I interject. "My sister, Gretel."

Colt shoots an aggravated look my way and covers the microphone, "This is not a secure line. This is a message to everyone. We weren't supposed to reveal her identity. Or say her name. That could put her in peril."

"What?" I ask. He points to the microphone. I cover the microphone and whisper, "I thought only the resistance would listen to this."

"Shush." He places a finger over his lips. "Are we telling them that the ambassador lives?"

I shake my head. Aunt Sandra motions to us. "Stay on script."

"Sorry about that, technical difficulties." Colt begins again attempting to explain the dead air. "Like we were saying, the resistance does indeed have a cure. The vaccine is being sent to every person. We will make sure that all of the people fighting for freedom get inoculated first."

"Then we will be sending the cure to everyone." I look at my script now trying to follow every word exactly. "There will be no charge. We don't want to withhold the vaccine from anyone. We want to make sure that the virus is gone forever."

I pass the script back to Colt, who continues, "Make sure those in remote areas make it to your rendezvous points to take the cure. It is nothing more than a vial of medicine. There are no side effects."

Once again, Colt slides the paper back in front of me. "The best part of the vaccine is that after two days it takes effect and you can no longer get the virus. You are immune forever. We plan to make this world ours again. No one will ever be called an Undesirable or an Uncounted. This is our world. We will make sure everyone has a voice."

Aunt Sandra and Colt nod.

Colt and I say at the same time. "Power to the resistance!"

The address ends and the microphone goes silent.

Colt and I hug.

"How did I do?" I ask.

Aunt Sandra says, "You two are strong leaders. I am hopeful. We might just have a chance to win this war."

I roll the four-leaf clover in my hand as I silently make my only wish: that Riley was here.

Chapter 8

Gretel shakes me awake. "Paisley! Wake up!"

"What?" I rub the sleep out of my eyes. "What do you want?"

Gretel sits on the side of my bed. "Colt wants to see you in the radio room. He said to hurry."

Swinging my legs over the side of the bed, I jerk my head. "What time is it? Did something happen?"

"I don't know." Gretel lets out a big breath. "He wouldn't tell me. He said he couldn't talk to me about it." She looks at me, cheeks flushing with urgency. Why is she upset? She throws my jeans at me and says, "You just need to go."

Tugging on my jeans, I fling my sleep shirt off and pull the fleece wear over my head. "I'm sure it's nothing." I knock into her shoulder. "Don't worry, whatever he tells me, I'll tell you. You know that."

She embraces me. "I knew you would say that. I knew you would tell me. Sisters don't keep secrets." She puts her finger on her chin. "Definitely tell me, unless it's a present or something like that. I do like surprises."

I roll my eyes. Why would Colt drag me up at dawn to tell me about a surprise present for my sister? I like that her work as a lab rat has kept her sheltered from a lot of the ugliness of war. Her mind is in the books and science; the death doesn't seem to register with her. Still, she witnessed our mother's public execution on television along with me and about a million other people.

I pull on my boots and follow my sister. She chatters all the way to the radio building about nothing. I barely listen. She drops me off at the door. "I'm not allowed to come in. He actually said that to me. Can you believe it?" I pat her on the back and give her a half-smile. I had to wake up for this drama? Go figure. I open the door and go inside.

Colt is slumped forward. The expression on his face tells me everything I need to know. This is something serious. I ask, "What happened?"

"Gretel is being targeted." His voice is low. Sweat trickles down his cheek.

"Why?"

His glare pierces my soul. It's because of me. My sister is in danger and it's my fault. I was so proud of my sister that I said her name over the airwaves last night.

Tears well. "It's because I gave them her name. I'll never forgive myself if she is hurt because of me."

"Calm down. I'm not going to let her out of my sight." He grabs my hand. "I know you didn't do it on purpose. But I don't want to scare her so I'm not going to tell her and you can't tell her either."

"I can't keep this from her. I appreciate you telling me first. But it's important for her to know the danger she is in." I take a deep breath. "How did you find this out? Tell me everything."

Colt bites his lower lip. "Last night the radio operator woke me up to come and hear the broadcast. When I arrived at the radio building, Oliver told me the chatter was that since Gretel knows how to make the cure that she is the number one "get." She is priority one and they are to make sure that the emperor has her as soon as possible."

"The emperor is in possession of one of the machines. They need the machine to manufacture the cure. He needs her to work it." Colt shakes his head. "It must be a replica of the machine that Gretel clamors on about being delicate and rare. If it's so rare, how did they get ahold of it? When they heard her name, somebody remembered her as being the ambassador's assistant. They put out a description and everything."

"And it's all because I mentioned her on the radio? Go ahead you can say it. I know it already. I've put my sister in danger."

"Forget about fault and focus on their plan." Colt continues, "The plan is that they get her. I know the compound is safe, but what if they follow a courier back here?"

He pauses for a second before continuing, "They hope that without her the resistance can't make more of the cure. They plan to make Gretel work for them." He sighs. "I'm worried. The royals and Mercs are desperate and desperate people do crazy things. We have to protect her."

"The best way to protect her is to let her know what's going on." I shift in my seat. "You said that you are going to make sure that you keep an eye on her all of the time." I turn my head from side to side. "If that is true, where is she?"

"I don't know what I was thinking. I'm her husband and I just want to protect her." He jumps up. "She won't know to be on the lookout for trouble if she doesn't know about it."

"She was going to the lab." I head for the door. "Let's go and tell her together."

As we exit the radio room, people scurry about. This is unusual. At this time of morning, everyone is usually at his or her assigned stations. Amanda crosses in front of us. I ask, "Amanda, what is going on?"

Amanda stops. "They sounded the alarm. Didn't you hear it?"

I hear it now. The bells are ringing.

She continues, "Someone has breached the outer realm of the maze. Everyone is scrambling to find out who it is."

"That's impossible. It has to be a hoax." Colt grabs her arm. "Wait. Where's Gretel?"

Amanda looks around. "I haven't seen Gretel." Colt releases his grip and she scampers off.

"This doesn't sound right. There is no way anyone found this compound. Something is very wrong." Colt looks at me. "Let's go to the lab and get Gretel first."

"I agree."

The two of us zigzag in and out of people running all around. The army of children is perched around the compound. A few have guns pointed at the opening of the maze.

"Did you see that the children are armed?" I shriek as we turn the corner toward the lab.

Colt's face is tortured. "Not now. First, Gretel."

I nod. He's right.

In a few minutes, we make it to the lab.

"Gretel!" Colt rushes in the door yelling. "Gretel, where are you?"

A lab worker is measuring some liquid into a vial. "She just left. No one came for the new batch of the cure set to go on a ship to South America. She took a bag of cures to deliver to the new couriers."

I ask, "What new couriers?"

The lab worker pushes his glasses to rest on the bridge of his nose, pulls his latex gloves off his hands with a loud popping sound, and tosses them in the trash. "The message. I thought you sent it. It was here when she got back." The lab worker shifts some papers around.

Colt's eyes get huge. "I didn't send anything. You have to find that note." He grabs the lab worker by his collar and spits as he talks. "Where's my wife?"

"Stop it!" I pull Colt off the bespectacled man.

The man shifts his collar around. It takes him a couple of seconds to compose himself again. "I said I'd find it for you. No reason to manhandle me."

"Sorry." Colt mumbles.

A few minutes later, the lab worker produces a paper. "Here it is."

Colt studies the note. "It did come from our office."

I grab the message. "What does it say?" I flip it over. "And when was it sent? Weren't you at the radio room?"

"I was there all morning." He stops for a moment and puts his hands on his hips. "Wait a minute, I left to tell her to get you. It must have come through then."

I run out the door. "C'mon we need to get up with Oliver. They have to be the ones who sent it."

Colt runs after me. "You go do that. I need to find Gretel." His eyes scan the compound. "I'll be there as soon as I can. Call Oliver and find out what's going on there."

My feet pound the dirt as I run back to the radio room. The operator is still there. I ask, "Did you take this message?"

He reads it aloud: *Virus cure that was on its way to South America has been destroyed. Please send more. I will meet you at Paisley's farm.*

"Yes." He hands the note back to me. "It was received this morning."

"Move over." I grab the microphone. "Oliver, come in." I stop for a moment. I'm not supposed to use his name. I'm supposed to use our code names. PACO. It's a mix of our names, Colt and me. PA for Paisley and CO for Colt. I start again. "PACO calling."

Oliver's voice comes on. "SONOL here." SONOL is Oliver's code. Son-Oliver.

I begin. "We received a message this morning which reads: Virus cure that was on its way to South America has been destroyed. Please send more. I will meet you at Paisley's farm. Did you send that?"

His voice booms into the speaker. "No. Paisley's farm home has been compromised. Make sure that no one goes there. They must have hacked our system. Did they use the SONOL code?"

Looking over at the radio operator, I know the answer before I ask him.

"Can't find her." Colt throws open the door and enters the room out of breath.

The boy in the radio room sinks his head in his hands. "I didn't think anyone else had the capability to use our radio system."

"I didn't think so either, but the message has been delivered." I release the button for a moment and then hold it down again to deliver the bad news. "The message was delivered to the lab."

"Why?" Oliver asks.

"Were you told to deliver it to the lab?" A feeling of despair overcomes me as I look over at the radio operator.

His shoulders droop. "I was told to deliver it to Gretel."

"Oh no." I let go of the microphone.

Colt gasps.

Oliver's voice booms. "We all heard all of that. You are to stay put. We will figure it out from here."

Colt bolts out of the doorway. I press the button again. "Too late. Her husband heard it all and is gone."

Riley's voice sounds. "My friend, you stay. I'll go after him. I promise I'll bring him home okay." Silence. Riley whispers, "I promise to bring them both back home."

Chapter 9

In the next few minutes, the radio operator delivers a message to the compound about Gretel's disappearance and the danger she is in. It doesn't take long for Aunt Sandra to show up. Aunt Sandra talks back and forth on the radio trying to sort the details. Amanda attempts to keep me calm.

Aunt Sandra pats my shoulder, "You and Amanda write everything that has happened this morning word for word. Don't leave anything out."

Write the whole thing up? Is she nuts? It's Aunt Sandra's rule. We don't want to miss anything. We must record all acts, mistakes, and successes. She says knowing our mistakes will help us not repeat them. But now? My initial reaction of rage slowly changes to calm. The writing seems to make me feel better. At least I have something to do. Aunt Sandra is so much wiser than me.

I'm worried about Riley and Colt. But I'm mostly scared for my sister. We can't find her anywhere. Aunt Sandra has scores of people scouring the countryside for her. A group is sent to try to join Colt in his quest to intercept Gretel before she gets to our farm.

Gretel knows all of the back ways to the farm. This is the farm that we grew up on. I wish I could have told her about the tunnels. She might have used them. If I had had time to tell Colt, he definitely could have used them. Everyone is scattered; even Riley is somewhere looking for Colt and my sister. My sister's in trouble because she is a good person trying to save people.

The sitting and waiting is killing me and now Aunt Sandra has insisted that I go on the air to rally the troops. I don't feel like it. Not at all.

After communicating back and forth with Oliver all day, the only thing he can tell me for sure is that Riley has left. There will be no way to reach any of them until they radio us. Most likely that won't happen until they return or find a resistance camp.

I'm so tired I doze off for a minute in the chair in radio room. I dream Gretel is unharmed and in one of the caves. She is eating pears and laughing at us for being so concerned. The next minute I am soaring on my Ferris wheel. I feel the wind in my face. I am peaceful and happy. I wake to see Aunt Sandra's face as she sits quietly beside me.

"This is SONOL. Come in PACO." The noise breaks my serenity.

Grabbing the microphone, I hear Oliver's voice.

I say, "PACO here. Any news."

"No." Another squawking noise. "Are you going on the air tonight?"

"Yes." I pause. "Alone." I place the microphone down.

My father's voice breaks in. "We need you now more than ever. The media blitz is bad. The Mercs think they can find the one they seek. We need to keep morale up. You represent hope. You have to keep the resistance forces in a positive frame of mind. Please. Let's make sure that we do this right."

I push the button again. "I wish I knew Gretel was okay."

My father's voice again. "Don't use her name please. The Mercs have developed a new device that specifically searches for names. Oliver thinks that is how they were able to hack in last night."

My heart sinks. I suspected it, but now I know. I tipped them off about Gretel. It is my fault that my sister might be killed. I have to make this right. I push the button again. "I'll be on at the regular time." I release the button. I can't let everyone down. I will do what a good soldier has to do. I won't be happy about it and my heart won't be into it, but I won't let anyone else know. My shoulders slump and I place my hands on my cheeks.

"We have to believe everything will work out." Aunt Sandra pats the back of my head. "Stay positive."

It's time. I sit in front of the microphone and shift it to "on." The lights flash on and off.

Aunt Sandra introduces me. "Tonight you have a treat. Colt is off on assignment. So we will have our Paisley to talk to us." She looks at me. "Paisley?"

"Hello resistance." I take a breath. "This is Paisley. I know that I'm supposed to tell you a story about Colt and me. About an adventure that we had and how we were able to get out of it. I know those adventure stories are fun and I know how they cheer you up."

I pause. "But tonight I want to talk to you about something real. I want to tell you about just a few of the people who have died trying to fight for our cause, for freedom. These people have given their lives to make sure that the rest of us have a shot at democracy."

Aunt Sandra smiles.

"One of those brave people was someone I met on the ship that Colt and I were on. An Undesirable. This Undesirable was more desirable than anyone I had ever known. He was the leader of the bottom floor of this ship. He made sure everyone had something to eat. He put others before himself and he tried to make everyone smile." A tear rolls down my cheek.

"He was a father. He was a brother. He was a husband. He was thrown off the ship because the king thought that he carried the virus. But more than that, he died because he was thought of as a lesser person. A person who could be owned and given orders. He was expendable or so they said. I don't believe this man was expendable. He was needed by his friends and family, but most of all he was needed by his children." I wipe my tear.

"I loved this man and I want to make sure that when we're finally free, we remember each and every one who gave the ultimate sacrifice for all of us."

I take in a labored breath. "Another of those brave people was a child. She was no more than ten years old. She gathered intel for our group. She never did anything wrong." I choke back more tears. "When she learned about the raid on my farm, she tried to make it back with that information. She was found barely alive and held on long enough to get her message to us. I owe her my life. She saved us all. She does not have a family. She was an Uncounted. But I'm here to tell you that the resistance was her family. We were all her brother, sister, aunt, uncle and mother and father. We love her because she was one of us."

"Another brave person was the bodyguard sent to protect me from the raid on the farm. He not only saved me," I clasp my hands together. "He pushed through a fatal injury to make sure that I survived. He said it was an honor to meet me. I say instead that it was an honor to meet him. He gave his life for me. He was my brother and your brother too."

"This is not the kind of uplifting message you were expecting tonight, but this message is real. This threat is real and if we don't do something now to stop this, then more of our brothers and sisters will die."

I puff out my chest and take in a deep breath. "The rest of us will forever live in a world in which we are owned and ordered around. We will be bought and sold like livestock. When we get too old or if we are hurt or if we are deemed by someone in power to be no longer useful we will be killed as if we are insects. We cannot let that happen. We must win. We must be strong. We are stronger together than we will ever be apart."

Alone, I raise my fist, "Power to the Resistance."

After I shut down the microphone, I hear applause. The radio room is filled with the people of the compound.

Aunt Sandra's eyes are brimming. "That was the most loving tribute ever given for the lost ones. You are truly a special person."

Amanda hugs me.

It's a struggle to get out of the chair. I'm exhausted. I find my way through all of the well-wishers. They pat me on the back.

"Wonderful." One of the trainees squeezes my hand.

Tears flow down an older lady's cheeks. "She was talking about Kelley."

A man nods his head. "I knew Charles. What a nice tribute."

"We should make a memorial wall or something for the people who have passed away." Aunt Sandra says to a passer-by.

"Everyone is important." A man with a pronounced limp shakes another man's hand who says, "I agree. She's right, we must win this war."

Amanda claps her hands together. "If we don't do something about it now, then the world will be lost forever."

Applause thunders throughout the compound as I make it back to my quarters and crawl into bed fully clothed. I am almost asleep when I hear Amanda. "Paisley, get up. There's news."

On the way to the radio room, I beg under my breath. "Please be good news. Please be good news."

As I enter, I hear my father's voice reporting on the radio. "The emperor has captured Gretel."

Chapter 10

My sister Gretel. I want to scream. I want to climb through the wires and choke the emperor, but I know I can't. I have to remain calm. I sink down in my chair for a moment unable to speak. My sweet sister is in the hands of the monstrous emperor.

I speak softly into the microphone. "How…"

My father's voice booms. "We are monitoring the situation. There are two heading to her location to try to free her. Will let you know as soon as possible what happens."

"Okay." It's all I can manage to get out.

"Your radio message to the troops was wonderful tonight. You should be so proud."

"Thanks." Once again, I can't get any more words out.

His voice softens, "Are you okay?"

Even though I try, I can't stop the tears. I did not notice Aunt Sandra in the back of the room. She comes to the microphone and presses the button. "We'll be okay here. PACO over and out."

She shuts down the microphone and sits beside me. I weep until I can't cry anymore. I don't know what to do. I can't think straight. My mind wanders from fear for my sister to the realization that we have lost our only way to make the cure. What if the emperor sells the cure? I don't think they will kill my sister. She's too important. She is the only person alive who can make the cure. Even the emperor wouldn't risk losing that.

My thoughts go to Riley and Colt. They will certainly make sure that they do everything to save her. What if they are killed trying to rescue her? Why am I only thinking of the most horrible things? I want a positive thought. I search for one, but nothing. I fear all is lost.

I slump in the chair unable to move and I cry myself to sleep.

My eyelids flutter awake. I'm in my bed in my room. I peek under the sheet and I'm fully clothed so someone must have carried me here. I go to the bathroom, wash my face, and brush my teeth. A shower will help. No time to feel sorry for myself; I must formulate a plan to get Gretel back.

After I dress, I go to the laboratory. I want to feel close to my sister. When I walk to the lab, everyone I see gives me the poor pitiful look like I'm an Uncounted with a time set for my execution. I hate that look.

The flurry of activity in the science laboratory surprises me. What's going on? Did Gretel leave instructions so explicit that the technicians are able to copy her work? That fleeting thought makes me happy.

"Hey, want to help?" My father stands in a white coat holding a vial of what I can only assume is the cure.

At this moment, it doesn't matter how many people are in here or how many people see me. I run and hug him. I wonder what the other lab technicians must think of me and why I would be so close to the ambassador. They don't know that he is my father, and to be honest I really don't care what anyone thinks right now.

The action takes him by surprise, but he hugs me back and I cry again.

He strokes my hair. "It'll be all right. I'm sure that Riley and Colt will get Gretel back."

"How can they? They must have her guarded. Why didn't she wait to talk to Colt or me about the problem? Why couldn't Colt or I have gotten to her first before she received the fake message? If only she had stayed here for just a while longer, she would have known about the danger." I bury my head on his shoulder and sob. "She thought everything was fine. She left thinking that she was helping; my heart aches with what ifs. I hate what ifs. If only Colt had told her they were looking for her. She might have been more careful." My voice breaks. "If only I hadn't said her name over the broadcast."

"Don't blame yourself." My father puts his finger to my lips. "No looking back, only looking forward. We must be positive. The best way to keep our minds off it is to stay busy. It's important that we keep busy."

"You're right." I wipe my eyes and take in a calming breath. "What are you doing here and when did you get here?"

"After you went to bed last night, Aunt Sandra and I talked on the radio. We decided it was paramount to keep up our manufacturing of the cure. Lives depend on it. I travelled here last night to keep our manufacturing on track."

I smile. "I'm glad you're here."

Picking up a beaker, he looks around. "I was truly surprised by this place. I had no idea it was here." He picks up a microscope. "They have managed to collect some state of the art equipment for this lab." He places the microscope back down. "Not sure how they collected some of the more modern devices. But I'm not going to question it. Aunt Sandra has done a great job hiding it all of these years. We did decide it's important to make sure that more than just a couple of people know how to make the cure."

"Is that why all of these people are here?" I turn in place looking at the full room. I see Amanda, Thomas, and Mike. "Are you also teaching the children?"

He nods. "I'm instructing anybody who is interested in learning. The more people who know how to manufacture it, the less chance we have of actually having an outbreak."

"Here." He sits in a chair and rolls another toward me motioning for me to sit down.

"What about Lieutenant Drake? I thought you were his right hand man." I take a seat. "What will he do without you and Riley there?"

"He has Oliver." He takes in a deep breath. "Although Oliver is more an intellect, not a fighter. And you are right about Riley. He's great at battle strategy. But it seems that there is another captain coming over from America."

"America?" This perks my interest. "What's his name?"

My father smiles. "Captain Via and he is a she."

Captain Via. I can't contain my reaction as I make a high squeaky noise.

"Do you know her?" My father asks.

I slow my breathing, calming my excitement. What if I'm telling my father about my mother? A few seconds pass before I'm able to speak without giving away my secret thoughts. "Yes, I met her when I was in America. She is the captain who introduced me to Eddie. She helped me return to Bavaria. She's great."

His comments are monotone as if he is talking about nobody special. "I've heard nothing but good things about her. I've never met her. From what I understand, she has a lot of knowledge about the virus and its cure. I am very thankful that she is able to come over to us. Oliver has been communicating with her."

"Ambassador..." One of the lab assistants taps my father on the shoulder. "I don't quite understand this step."

"I'll be there in a minute." My father pats me on the arm. "You sit here as long as you like. I need to show as many as I can about how to manufacture and mix the cure. It's important."

He walks over to the students, patiently explaining each step of how to mix the virus.

How wonderful that Captain Via is coming over from America. I would love to be there when they meet. My brother will be working with her. I could be wrong but I just know that she is my mother, my real mother, my birth mother. The only proof I have is a distinct birthmark on her neck. I can't tell my brother that he is my brother and I can't tell my maybe mother that she could be my mother and I can't tell my father about my maybe mother. It is so mixed up. But for the last few minutes I haven't once thought of Gretel, Riley, or Colt. And maybe just for today, that is a good thing.

Thomas, Amanda, Mike, and I learn how to mix the virus cure. It's not hard provided you know the basics. The cure is synthesized from blood.

My father winks at me when he introduces the blood. "This is your blood that we used to make the DNA strand." Fortunately, my father has invented a replicating machine that strips the DNA out of anyone's blood. The DNA voided blood then passes through his device and replicates another's DNA strand.

For the cure, the machine replicates a synthetic form of my blood which contains the antibodies needed to immunize the populace from the virus. Actually, after seeing this I wonder if Gretel will have any luck at duplicating the cure without all of this equipment or any of my blood.

"How many of these replicators are there?" Mike asks my father as he holds up a vial, swirling its contents.

"A least a hundred," My father answers, "This is what I did for the military. This is the machine I was hired to invent."

Thomas pours a beaker full of fluids and measures it out in a test tube. "Why would the military want this type of machine? What could it be used for?"

Amanda shouts, "The only thing I can think of is for bioterrorism."

My father's face goes ashen. Did he know that this science was slated for use as a bioterrorism weapon? Is that what he had been working on all those many years ago? A weapon? The thought of it turns my stomach.

He completely ignores Amanda's comment and goes back to explaining the steps involved in making the virus cure. I don't press for an answer. Not sure if I want to hear it.

At first, the time ticks off the mounted clock slowly, but as I get better at the procedure, the hours fly by. I see Baako on my way back to the bunking area after the day is over.

Baako kicks some dirt as he walks by. "I think we should go and get Gretel. We've been training for just such a thing."

My heart leaps. Another who wants to *actually* do something? "Sure," I whisper. "But we have to make a plan. We can't just storm out of here, walk onto the ship, and get her."

He smiles. "So you've been thinking about rescuing her."

"She's my sister." I sit on a bench near the drawbridge. "Of course I have. I've thought of practically nothing else, but we need a plan."

Baako sits beside me, nudging me with his shoulder. "Luckily, I have a plan."

Chapter 11

I want Gretel back so badly that I don't press Baako for the specifics of his plan. I just follow him. I know it's dangerous to leave the compound, but I have to try to save Gretel.

It doesn't seem right that only the men and boys are expected to go into the dangerous situations. I've been in plenty of difficult situations. I do it because I have to. This is one of those "have to" times. I want my sister back unharmed.

Knowing that sneaking off will not be easy, Baako and I grab some essentials and throw them in a backpack. I grab a scarf of Gretel's and a sock of Colt's from their room before I leave. Might need their scent to track. It is so dark.

Baako says he knows where a couple of sentry uniforms are. The sentries dress differently so they can be identified easily. I follow him to the laundromat. Smart thinking. We find the extra uniforms, change quickly, and throw on our backpacks.

We need weapons. I take Baako to the area where we train our army of children. We gather as many dirt bombs and sling shots as we can carry. We take care not to weigh ourselves down, as that would defeat the purpose of being stealth.

The uniforms get us quickly and invisibly out of the compound and through the maze. The sentries ignore us as we grunt through. They most likely think that we are extra guards as Aunt Sandra made a big announcement about adding more security for the compound.

After passing through the entrance gate without any trouble, we travel to our hidden pasture. Baako picks a horse and Hershey nuzzles me when he sees me. I pull a couple of apples out of my backpack to give to each of our horses. We feed the animals and then we are off.

It will take all night to reach Hamburg.

Baako's plan involves finding Tury. Tury and Baako have a special relationship. They were saved together after being thrown off the ship. Thank goodness Colt and I were able to save them!

A simple plan. We get off the compound. Done! We make our way to Hamburg. On our way! We get on the ship and find Tury. Hopefully that will be as easy to accomplish as the rest. Baako thinks that Tury will know where Gretel is.

It might not be the best or most thought out plan, but I don't have a better one. It's certainly better than just sitting here doing nothing. My father and everybody else on this compound will be very upset in the morning when they find out we're gone. I can't worry about that now. I'm on a mission to save Gretel.

The trail is treacherous at night, full of many places to fall and break our necks. If we happen upon a stray Merc or two, it's certain death. Thank goodness, Hershey knows her way. I give her a smell of Colt's sock, after which she tracks his scent all the way to Hamburg. That book about equine air scenting is paying off.

We hit Hamburg early in the morning just before sunrise. The hills that had been hidden by the navy black now explode with orange hues. We are no longer cloaked by darkness.

Baako pulls at his sentry clothes. "We need a better disguise."

I smile. "Let's hide the horses first. Don't worry, I have an idea."

We leave Hershey and the other horse safely behind in the woods. Far enough away to not be easily found, yet close enough that we can get back to them.

As the morning dawns in Hamburg, I notice a familiar store. It's the "Sponsored Companions" store. Ms. DeVane won't be there. She is off with her son fighting the good fight for the resistance side.

"Where are we going?" Baako asks.

I lead him down barren streets. It's so early that not even the bread stores are open.

Standing in front of the doll store, memories flood my mind and I lose my breath for a moment. This store helped Colt and I gain access to the ship the first time. Could it be lucky for me again? It's been a while; at least it's still in business.

"It's too early. It's not open." Baako says.

He follows as I make my way around back, carefully hiding in the shadows. "We don't want it to be open."

Baako's eyes widen. "Are we going to break in?"

"Sort of."

I walk to the entry door of the adjacent store. "The doll store is actually connected to another store that's not in business anymore. That shop is used as storage.

I'm hoping that we can get in that way. Wouldn't that be great?"

"It would be a miracle." Baako's eyes widen in amazement as he watches me jiggle the doorknob.

It's old and offers little resistance. I open the unlocked door. "I can't believe it."

"Hurry." I shove him in front of me through the door and pull it closed behind me. "We don't want to be seen."

We climb over the junk and debris and come to another entry. I hold my breath. "The back of the store is through this entrance."

"Can our luck still hold out?" Baako laughs.

I twirl the four-leaf clover and pull on the doorknob. Sure enough, this door opens also. No jiggling needed, it's not even locked. Now safely inside the store, I let out a big breath.

The large storeroom is divided by beams and an archway. The far side of the room is full of hanging clothes, men's and women's of all shapes and sizes, but all basically the same design. A life-size poster reading "Sponsored Companions," stands on the far side of the room. The rest of the room is populated with dolls and doll clothes.

Baako sits on a chair in the store. "What are we looking for and what exactly is the plan?"

"You do remember what my "Sponsored Companion" outfit looked like, don't you?" I flip through the hanging clothes. "I'm looking for the dress that matches the Norwegian doll. See?" I point to a large poster advertising the Norwegian doll as coming soon.

"Oh." Baako smiles with recognition. "Do all Europeans dress alike?"

"Guess so." I pull a Norwegian outfit out to study. The outfit consists of a black skirt, black tights, white apron, finished off with the red bib with the rickrack embellishments of ribbon along the edge. I put on the red hat. Best of all, the shoes are black and flat and look comfortable. I hand Baako the male equivalent. "This is the newest doll's clothes. Let's hope the princess doesn't has them yet."

"I get it now. Where do I change?" Baako asks.

Along the back wall, I open another door. "Here's a bathroom. Put these clothes on. Then I'll do the same. Don't take too long."

Baako reappears in a few minutes, pulling at the white tights and knee length black pants. He also dons a vest and shirt. After he puts on his shoes, his outfit is complete. He admires his reflection in the mirror, posing in the tailored jacket, and cocks his head commenting, "I make this look good."

I slip into the bathroom and change. Unzipping my backpack, I grab my other clothes. "Let's put the sentry outfits into our backpacks in case we need them later." Baako does the same. With the exception of the missing outfits, we leave no trace.

We're ready. We exit the store the same way we came in: through the back entrance, being careful not to disturb anything.

Finding a way onto the ship might prove to be difficult, but walking down the street is easy. The streets are still vacant, no people milling around.

"Are they hiding because they believe the virus is making a comeback?" Baako asks.

I stop walking. "Maybe." I had not thought of that.

He continues, "We might not be able to get on the ship. What are we going to do if we can't?"

"We're going to find a way." I cock my eyebrow. Did he think we would come all of this way and not try anything and everything to get on the ship?

A strong feeling of relief overcomes my senses when the ship comes into view. "Look." I nod my head toward the massive vessel. The original name, "Queen Mary IV," had been written with raised letters that could not be completely erased. It has been consigned to rest as a shadow beneath a new moniker in bolder brighter lettering. A name I know, "Queen Nalani."

People scurry about pulling ropes and polishing railings and banisters, anything tied or not tied down. I twirl the four-leaf clover again. We need all of the luck we can get.

"C'mon Baako." My hand clutches Baako's arm. "And please act like you belong." I strut a couple of steps, pulling him along. "Be confident. They can smell fear every time."

Baako trembles. "But I am scared."

The ship's gangplank is down. No one pays any attention to us. So far so good.

It can't be this easy.

I was right.

The sentry at the gate yells, "Halt! Who goes there?"

Chapter 12

"We are the new Norwegian "Sponsored Companions" sent for Princess Kamea. We just arrived," I rattle on. I squeeze Baako's arm since he is shaking so much. At least he is smart enough to know not to say a word.

The sentry questions my announcement. "I haven't heard about any new dolls. I'm going to need verification."

I open my mouth to protest.

"Silence. I have to call Miss Brita and find out what's going on."

Miss Brita. We might have a chance. I am relieved that Miss Brita is still in service to the queen. She knows me and she knows Baako. She might let us pass.

It's a gamble, but one I am willing to take to save my sister.

Baako doesn't move. I know he recognizes the name of Miss Brita too. We wait for our fate.

It seems like an eternity before Miss Brita arrives. A large burly man pushes her in a wheelchair. I had hope that she would make a full recovery from a gunshot wound she'd endured during a botched attempt on the ambassador's life. I remember that scary day. We are all lucky to have survived it. She does not look well.

"What is this about sponsored comp..." She stops mid-sentence when she sees us. "Oh yes, those "Sponsored Companions." She looks us over. "Remind me, where are you from again?"

I curtsy. "Norwegian "Sponsored Companions." We're new."

Miss Brita motions to the sentry. "Let them pass."

We follow Miss Brita and the man who is pushing her onto the main deck of the all too familiar ship. We're quiet. Can't say anything until we get her alone. Not sure who is friend or foe.

As we make our way onto the main part of the ship, I scan the deck. The emperor has changed a lot of the decor. The old art has been replaced. There is no longer the great oil painting of the king adorning the hallway.

Now a sculpture of the emperor riding a horse takes up most of the lobby area. The beautiful paintings of the queen and princess have been removed to make room for two paintings of the emperor. The servants are dressed shabbily, even Miss Brita. She always used to have every hair in place. Now her outfit is worn and frayed.

It seems the emperor is not only evil, he doesn't take care of those in his service. I make a mental note of that fact; it might become useful later as we search for a way to dethrone this self-appointed ruler.

All of these people need rescuing. This is what the resistance is all about. These people need to be able to choose the path of their own lives. The emperor is much worse than the king and the king was a monster. We have to save them all.

My thoughts are interrupted by the sound of Baako's teeth chattering with fear. I tighten my grip on his arm.

We arrive at the elevator and Miss Brita rolls herself in. "John, you can go. I'll take care of this myself."

Baako and I take our place in the elevator. John stands outside the elevator door and keeps it from closing. "Are you sure?"

She nods, he removes his hand, and the door closes.

"Well?" Miss Brita glares at me.

Ignoring the indignant tone in her voice, I release Baako, lean down, and hug her shoulders. "Oh my goodness, it's so good to see you."

Her facial features soften and she reaches an arm up to acknowledge my embrace. "I've missed you too." With her other arm she reaches for Baako. "And you, my dear."

Baako clutches her arm, his muscles relax, and he draws in a deep breath. His trembling subsides.

Miss Brita releases her grip. "What are you two doing here? Everyone is looking for you." She glances at Baako. "Well not you. They all think you're dead. I thought you were dead. Didn't you get thrown into the ocean?"

"Long story." Baako tips his head and doesn't offer an explanation.

Miss Brita turns her attention to me. "Why are you here?"

Without taking a breath, I explain about how Gretel was kidnapped and how we think she is on board the ship. I also share with Miss Brita how the resistance lied about the virus and that it's not out again, but that we do have a cure.

"Miss Brita, we have a vial of the cure, you should take it." Baako pulls a vial from his backpack. "We don't want you to get the virus." He holds the small tube out to her.

She carefully reaches out for the miracle vial. "I didn't really believe that you had found the cure. I heard rumors. But with the ambassador dying. I thought the ability to protect ourselves from the disease went with him." She gazes for a moment at the ceiling. "He was a great man. I miss him so much."

I couldn't tell her that my father, the ambassador, was still alive. That knowledge could get her killed.

She cradles the vial in her hand. "So this is all we needed to stop that horrible disease from ravaging the world."

"You thought of everything, Baako. I had a bunch of those vials sitting in my room and I didn't think once about bringing them." I smile at him.

"I know. I saw them in your room when we packed." Baako shuffles his feet. "I thought, why not? We might need them."

I slap him lightly on the arm. "You got them all?"

Baako nods, with a slight grin.

I smile. "Good thinking."

Miss Brita rocks the vial gently in her hands. "I'm not sure I can accept this. How could I ever repay you?"

I interrupt, "That is what the resistance is all about. It's free. Please take it and then that is one less worry for you."

"Thanks." She gulps it down in one swallow. "Better not leave it out or throw it in the trash. Might cause someone to ask questions." She hides the empty vial in her pocket. "Now tell me what you are doing here."

I'm not able to answer as the elevator reaches its destination and the door opens.

"Come with me." Miss Brita rolls her wheelchair out. "There's a free room at this end of the hall." She wheels herself down to the end of the corridor. "This one."

Baako opens the door. "This takes me back. I remember this room." He playfully knocks into my shoulder. "Some good memories, not all bad."

This is one of the staterooms we stayed in before while we were in service to the queen and the princess as "Sponsored Companions." I take a second to glance around before I flop on the mattress. "We are here to find my sister Gretel." I pat the bed to clue Baako to sit beside me.

Miss Brita locks her wheels in place. "I haven't seen Gretel. Are you sure that she is here?"

"Is the emperor here?" I cock my head.

"Of course." Miss Brita lets out an exasperated breath. "He doesn't let the royals out of his sight. I think he is fearful that it's only their presence that ensures his reign." She shakes her head. "He's probably right."

"Tell us what has been going on." I stare at her. "What happened to the king?"

Miss Brita tightens up for a minute and white knuckles the arms of her chair.

"I don't want to upset you. If you don't want to tell me, it's fine. I'm just worried." I pause for a minute before continuing. "There is no love lost between me and the king. I was surprised when I heard that he was dead."

"Emperor Richard the Great swooped in soon after you left, Paisley." Miss Brita folds her hands in front of her lap. "Right after we heard that the ambassador had been killed."

She pauses for a minute before continuing. "He managed to marry the queen before she gave birth. I don't blame the queen. She was in a weakened state and then the emperor took her father from her."

I grab her folded hands. "Did he actually kill the king?"

She clears her throat. "The only thing I know is one minute the king is vibrant and the next he is sick and the next he is dead." She leans over and whispers, "I think he might have been poisoned."

"That would make sense. Not a quick death or a messy murder. The emperor is smart," I whisper. "He probably used a slow poison."

That would follow the timeline Miss Brita had just explained. If the emperor had indeed poisoned the king, then it would have taken awhile for him to get sick and finally succumb to the deadly drug.

I squeeze her hands for a moment. "I'm sorry for your loss. I know you've been in service with the king and queen for a very long time." I pause another minute. "Go on, Miss Brita, tell us the rest. What is going on now?"

She shakes her head. "I'm worried about the queen and the children. The emperor doesn't need them anymore to gain the power. He never goes and visits them. He ignores them completely. I am in charge of their food intake. We have one cook who brings them their meals and she is the only one who I will allow to give them food." She pauses and looks up as if she is trying to conjure up a memory. "Tury, that's the cook's name."

"Tury, she's one of us." Baako lights up and shifts his whole attention to Miss Brita. "We need to find her. She may be able to tell us if Gretel is here."

Miss Brita's lips purse. "I can do that, but why is Gretel so important?"

Baako starts. "She's the one who makes..."

"She's important because she's my sister." I interrupt. I glare at Baako. No reason to load Miss Brita down with information that could be used against her at some point.

"I didn't realize that. I'll keep a look out for them, but for now if you want to see Tury she will be delivering the food at 0900 to the playground location on the fifteenth floor." Miss Brita rubs her forehead.

"You rest. We can find her. I can see you're tired. You've done more than enough." I squeeze her hand. "Thanks, Miss Brita. We will take it from here."

She clasps my hand and Baako's. "What will you do now?"

I let go of her hand. "It's best that you don't know. If we're caught, we will protect you until our last breath. I promise you that."

Her face contorts. "Goodness, I hope it doesn't come to that."

Baako nods. "Me too."

Miss Brita looks over her shoulder as she wheels herself out. "If I don't see you again...." She pauses. "Good luck and be careful." She pulls the empty vial from her pocket. "Thanks for this. Thanks for the cure. You've probably saved my life." She disappears down the corridor.

Baako and I sit quietly. He rubs his eyes. "We don't have anything to do until 0900. I don't know about you, but I'm tired. We might want to sleep at least an hour. It could be a very long day. Don't know when we'll get to sleep again. Because we might have to travel all night tonight too."

He's right. Fortunately, the bedroom cabin that Miss Brita put us in has a security lock. No one should be coming but if they do, there is another door to the outside hall that we can access by the connecting door. I set the alarm clock in the room for 0830 and we both curl up to sleep.

At 0845, we peek out the door into the corridor. All clear. We are fresh from our short nap and ready to get Gretel and escape before the morning crew awakes. We decide to take the stairs. It is easy to duck and hide while on stairs, but impossible on the elevator.

Trudging down the five flights, we are quiet and my adrenaline is pumping. I notice the elegant carpet on the stairs is more worn as the steps descend. The paintings that decorate the landings also deteriorate in value. The first flights, so embellished and rich looking with gold fluted frames are replaced with decorations, less ornate, until finally the paintings disappear completely. At the fifteenth floor, peeling wallpaper and stained carpet become the norm. I push a piece of wallpaper back in place.

I'm elated when we finally reach our destination. "Here it is. The playroom must be at the end of the corridor."

"Baako." A voice from behind us whispers.

Baako turns and almost knocks the tray out of the woman's hand. She steadies it before it falls. He hugs her, draping his arms over her back. "Tury. We're looking for you."

"Me?" She scrunches her face. "I'm happy here, I don't need to be saved."

"Did you give the children the cure?" Baako pulls out a cure vial and offers it to her. "Did you take it yourself?"

She shakes her head. "There were only two vials left. The "Sponsored Companions" took the rest. I think they were told to take the cure."

She is right. I remember that being the instruction. Of course, Tury would have been unselfish and made sure that everyone else got it before her. "When did the prince and princess get the cure?"

"I gave it to them two days ago." Tury takes the tube from his hand. "Is this extra? Did you come all this way to give me the cure?" Her eyes brim with tears.

Baako nods. "Good about the children because it takes two days for you to have an immunity from the virus." The food tray wobbles and Baako steadies it. "One of the reasons we came was to deliver you the cure. Take it now." He holds the tray while she throws her head backwards and gulps the medicine.

"I can't stay." She steadies the tray. "I have to feed the children. They will be looking for me soon if I don't deliver. I can't risk being late."

"Of course." I say, "Have you seen my sister Gretel?"

Tury leans in and whispers, "I'm not supposed to know she's here. But I accidentally heard talking about opening the ambassador's research laboratory. I saw a young woman with a bag over her head. From what I know about your sister that has to be her. She's a prisoner in the lab. The emperor is personally overseeing her captivity. That is not a good thing. If you want to save her you better hurry." She turns to Baako. "I'm so glad that you are well. Stay well. I have to go. Good luck."

"Thanks for taking care of the children." I say quickly.

She smiles. "Thanks for the cure." She disappears down the hall.

I turn to Baako. "Come on."

We travel the stairs two at a time until we see the big double doors marked "LAB." I put an index finger to my lips. We don't say a word. I lean up to peek through the glass at the top of the doors while Baako keeps a lookout. I don't see her, but I remember the room from the time the Mercs kept me and Colt imprisoned on that floor.

Suddenly I hear footsteps from inside the room near the door. Baako and I slide down the corridor and sink into an alcove.

The door flings open and two men bolt out. "I don't understand why we need all of this security for one little girl. She's so scared she's not going to try anything. It's crazy. Besides what's with all of the hazardous suits? You would think she had the virus."

"I'm just glad to get out of that binding contraption. I hate it." The other man says, "I don't care. I just do what I am told. Especially when they tell me it's important to wear that stuff. I'm going to listen. Where's our relief?"

Two other men enter from the stairs and meet them at the doorway entrance. On man says, "We're here. Any problems."

I whisper to Baako, "Must be their replacements."

One of the first men shakes his head. "Not a peep. If we didn't have to wear the biohazard suits, this job would be a piece of cake."

"Biohazard?" Baako whispers.

"We've been inoculated against the virus so we should be fine." I say softly.

It's not long before the original two disappear up the stairs. When the other two enter, the door swings back and forth. It's our chance–maybe our only chance to enter. We make a run for it.

We carefully slide through the doorway and sit quietly in a corner for a few seconds to see if we've been noticed. Nothing. We're home free.

All we have to do is find Gretel, knock out the guard, and make our way back safely to Aunt Sandra's compound. It's still a lot to accomplish. Never easy.

Scuffling sounds come from inside the room. I look at Baako. "Do you hear that?"

"Sounds like a fist fight," he whispers, "Don't move. Maybe we will be lucky and they'll knock each other out. Goodness knows we need some luck."

I twirl the four-leaf clover in my hand. Instinct to touch it any time luck is mentioned. I whisper, "What about Gretel?"

Baako pats his backpack. "We might be able to trade the cure for her release."

"Good thinking. It's worth a try." I take in a deep breath and we quietly come out from our hiding place to confront the Merc security.

We're right, there was a fight. Two Mercs are slumped over on the floor, unmoving. They are dressed in full body bio-suits. It's confusing. Two other men are standing over them, fists drawn. They wear regular security clothing. No bio-suits. Strange. The only good news is that we will only have to take out two of them. I look at Baako. "Ready?"

We run full force at the two Mercs. Baako locks his arms around one.

Abruptly, I stop. I see a familiar face.

Riley.

Chapter 13

"**P**aisley?" Riley throws his arms around me and squeezes.

I tip backwards before hugging him back. "What..."

"We haven't got time for this." Colt shoves Baako off of him and slaps my shoulder. "You shouldn't be here. We told you that we had it covered. We have to find Gretel." He points to a locked room in the back of the lab. "That has to be where she is." He glances at me quickly. "No time to talk. We'll talk later. Let's find her and get out of here."

"Agreed." I nod, release Riley, and motion toward the lab entrance door. "Baako, keep a lookout."

Riley, Colt, and I quietly sneak toward the locked room.

Colt whispers, "Gretel."

My sister's soft voice makes my heart skip a beat. "Colt?"

Colt's voice cracks. "She's here. Let's break the lock."

Baako steps forward. "Riley, go watch the door."

"What are you doing here?" I grab Baako's arm. "You're supposed to be the lookout."

"I can get in that door. I can break in."

"Let him try." Riley bolts to stand guard.

Baako places his backpack on the floor and pulls out a piece of wire. He puts the end of the wire in the lock and jiggles it. The pin tumblers lock in place and the knob turns.

Colt throws the door open and rushes in to Gretel. She's on the floor, a canvas bag covering her head as she struggles to right herself.

Colt wastes no time reaching his wife, cradling her as he pulls off the bag. "Gretel, I was so worried." He unties her hands and her feet and lifts her in his arms.

Tears run down her cheeks. "I knew you would find me."

I hug them both quickly. "Save this for later. We have to get out of here before we're caught."

"We can't go." Gretel digs her heels in the floor. "*I can't go.*"

Colt presses her head into his shoulder. "You're confused. You'll feel better when we get you back to Aunt Sandra's compound. It's not safe here. We have to go. I just don't know what would have happened..." His voice trails.

"The children." Gretel pushes her husband away. "We have to save the children."

"What children?" I turn Gretel to face me.

Gretel rubs her wrists. "The children, the prince and princess. They gave them the virus."

I cock my head. "What do you mean they gave them the virus?"

Colt pushes me forward toward the door as he guides Gretel through the room with Baako following behind.

Gretel whispers quickly, "What did you think the bio suits were for? They injected me with the virus to test the cure and make sure we weren't lying. Then they injected the queen and the two children. The emperor plans to use their deaths to incite the people against you and the rebels."

"Remind me." I inquire, "How long does it take the virus cure to take effect?"

Gretel trips, but grabs Colt's shoulder. "Twenty-four to forty-eight hours."

"The children will be fine." I put a hand on her arm. "Also, we gave Miss Brita the cure last night and Tury the cure this morning so they will be immune too."

Gretel claps her hands together. "Thank goodness the children will be saved. As long as Tury or Miss Brita weren't infected with the virus last night or this morning, they'll be fine. But the queen..." She wipes a tear from her cheek.

"Will the queen die?" I swallow the lump forming in my throat.

Gretel sniffs. "Yes and the emperor will know the children have been given the cure when they don't develop the virus. Tury and Miss Brita could be in danger too. We have to warn them. They have to come with us."

"We'll get them out." Colt holds his wife close. "Us. Not you." He gestures to Baako. "Take her to the horses."

Colt tugs Gretel's sleeve and motions to me. "Gretel, change clothes with Paisley. You and Baako should be able to slip out as "Sponsored Companions.""

I quickly pull off my skirt. The boys turn around. Really? Like I'm worried about modesty at a time like this.

"I'm not sure," Gretel protests. "I want to stay and help."

"My sweet wife, you have to make it back." Colt gently rubs her cheek. "You've been through enough. We can get them to safety without you. I can't risk losing you again. Besides, I can't think unless I know you are out of danger." He looks deeply into his wife's eyes. "I promise to get the children and the others to safety. I promise. Besides, we stand a better chance with less people. We'll be able to maneuver less conspicuously just a couple at a time. Trust me."

Gretel doesn't argue; I know that she knows Colt's right. Gretel and Baako change into the Norwegian "Sponsored Companion's" clothes.

Colt kisses his wife as she and Baako sneak out the door and up the stairs.

He turns to Riley and me. "Plan or any ideas?"

"What if you two, dress as security." I purse my lips. "And walk with me as if I'm a prisoner?"

"Might work." Riley nods. "Let's see if we can get to the fifteenth floor before Tury goes back to the kitchen."

"Wait a minute. I've got a better idea." Colt disappears and returns in a few minutes with a biohazard suit. "I found this one hanging beside the others. "

"I get what you're thinking." Riley snatches the suit and shoves it at me. "You dress in this one. Colt and I will take the other guards' suits. This ought to scare anyone we run into."

"A better plan," I say, "While I change, put one of the guards in Gretel's place." I pull off Gretel's skirt and sweater. "Here!" I throw the clothes at Riley. "Put these on the knocked out guard and cover his head with the sack. Rip them and place them over him. Just make sure that he is knocked out and gagged. Hopefully, no one will think she is gone. Might buy us some time."

Riley grabs the clothing mid-air. "Devious." He smiles. "We'll hide the other guard in a closet or something.

"Make sure the guards are securely tied up and gagged. We can't have them telling anyone about us." Colt puts on the guard's suit. "Let's hurry. Somebody might come in and we could be discovered any minute."

"Definitely." I help Riley pull one guard into a closet to hide and place the other guard in Gretel's place.

The three of us run down the stairs, Colt in front, me center, and Riley bringing up the rear. Two flights down, we see a man. He gasps as we get near. "Don't touch me!" He shouts and slams into the wall trying to avoid us.

"Wow." I laugh as we fly down the stairs. "This might work."

The outside door of the fifteenth floor is guarded by two men in biohazard suits. They must be worried about the contagion. Might should have thought of that before they purposefully started infecting people.

One of the men asks Colt, "Are you here to relieve us?"

Colt grunts, "Yes."

Great! Our plan is working. The men are excited to leave. Standing guard over a potentially contagious person is not a desired job. They waste no time disappearing up the stairs.

"I'll stay here." Riley peers at me through the plastic covering in his hood. "No offense, but you can't stay out here. We can't chance them getting a good look at you."

I pull at the front of my suit. "True."

Colt and I make our way back to the children's room. Tury is holding the little prince and soothing his soft cries while Miss Brita tries to calm down the princess who is sitting in her chair. Their eyes fill with fear when they see us.

Colt pulls off his hood and the children calm down. He says, "We need to get you out of here. The emperor gave the children the virus."

"What kind of a monster is he? How could he do that?" Miss Brita's tear streaked face looks up at Colt. "He said they had tested positive for the virus this morning. When he told me that they had contracted the virus from the resistance, I knew he was lying."

I remove my hood. "The emperor had them checked this morning?"

Miss Brita sobs holding the princess. "Yes, this morning."

"How?"

Miss Brita wipes a tear from her cheek. "A doctor gave them a vitamin shot this morning and then said they had the virus."

"That had to be the virus. Gretel said they were injected this morning. That's what all of the bio suits are for." Looking over at Colt, I say, "The emperor gave them the virus this morning."

A look of horror covers Miss Brita's face. "The vitamin injection was the virus?"

"Yes, but don't worry. I spoke with Gretel. The prince and princess have the immunity because they were given the cure in time. Thank goodness they're immune. You and Tury have been given the antidote so you will be immune in a couple of days."

Miss Brita's face is ashen. "A couple of days?"

"He didn't inject you, did he?" I take the princess from her as Miss Brita's arms go limp.

"This morning." Miss Brita takes in a deep breath. "I had no idea it was the virus. I thought it was a vitamin shot. The emperor's physician said it would help the children fight off diseases. I watched him inject the queen and the children. I thought it was safe. I was happy when he offered to inject me too."

Her eyes brim with tears. "I didn't realize it was actually the virus. I overheard the emperor and the doctor talking. I should have known." She strokes her fingers through the princess' hair. "I'm glad the children will live."

I look to Colt as my eyelids flutter to hold back tears. Too late. I swipe my cheek. "She could still survive."

"No way to defeat the virus once it is in your system." Colt's face loses its color. "The only way is to be immune."

Miss Brita leans down to the chair and kisses the princess's head. "She's fallen asleep. Please save them both. Tury has not been injected with the virus. She can help you get out. She knows the way."

Miss Brita kisses the curls of the prince as he cuddles in Tury's arms. "Tury, take them through the sixteenth floor. Go the back way. When you get there, walk down the gangplank used to bring supplies on." She turns to gaze at us. "Take off your bio suits and smuggle the children off in potato sacks. I'll distract them as long as I can."

"No!" I throw my arms around Miss Brita. "There must be another way."

"There isn't and you know it. Even if I wasn't doomed to die, I would slow you down because of this wheelchair." Miss Brita grips the wheels and smiles. "Paisley, I am proud to have known you. Your mission now is to save the children. The emperor will kill them if he finds out they survived the virus. There is nothing you can do for me. Go! It's my time to die. I know it and you know it."

Colt catches me as I sway, almost falling. She's right, but it's so hard to accept.

Tury stands up holding the prince. "Miss Brita, I promise to protect these children with my life. When they are old enough to understand, I will tell the children of your bravery and sacrifice. I will make sure they know the part you played in their escape."

Colt picks the princess from her chair as she starts to wake up.

I pull her from Colt. "Give her to me." I sit the princess back down on the chair. "Do you want to play a game with Paisley and Colt?"

The princess rubs the sleep out of her eyes and nods. "I missed you."

"We are going to play potato sack. Do you think that you can sit in a potato sack and not make a sound?"

"A game. Yea!" She squeals with delight.

"It's a race," I continue. "Guess who'll be carrying you?"

She looks around and I point to Colt. She squeals again.

Colt pats Miss Brita on the knee. "We have to go."

I hug Miss Brita one last time. Don't cry. Stick to the plan. We take off the top covering of the bio suit. I rip the pants to make them look more like work clothes. Colt tosses me his undershirt. Hope we look like we belong.

Tury carries the little prince and Colt, the princess. We meet Riley at the door and tell him about the plan and Miss Brita. He clenches his teeth as he pulls off his suit. He keeps a belt. We toss the rest of the discarded bio hazard garb into the fifteenth floor corridor maintenance closet.

Miss Brita rolls to the door. "When you leave, I'll bolt it behind you."

Miss Brita hugs Riley and he hands her the belt. "Wrap the belt from the bio suit around the handle. It will make it harder for them to open."

She clutches the belt.

"Sorry, Miss Brita." Riley's eyes fill.

"Don't worry I've seen this virus at work before. It won't be long. Maybe a day then I'll be free of this world." Miss Brita rolls her wheelchair back into the room and locks it in place.

My heart breaks. Tury leads as we travel down the stairs hopefully to find our freedom.

We enter the sixteenth floor and are surprised that there is no one there. Colt grabs up two potato sacks. "The children."

Tury carefully slides the prince into the bag while still carrying him like a baby. Colt grabs the princess and she gleefully lets him put her in the sack. She squeals with delight when he throws her over his shoulder. I spy a rag and tie it around my head similar to Tury's headdress. Not much of a disguise, but better than nothing.

No one stops us as we exit the gangplank; it seems that all of the guards have been dispatched elsewhere. Maybe the guards aren't expecting supplies and assume no one needs to guard the exit. I don't have the energy to figure out why it is not guarded. My heart is happy and sad all at the same time. Happy to be saving my half-brother and sister and sad that we couldn't save Miss Brita.

My mind wanders quickly to the image of the last time I will see or speak to Miss Brita. I glance one last time at the ship. Unfortunately, this escape is not without cost.

Chapter 14

We make our way quickly down the streets of Hamburg and back through the forest to where the horses are hidden.

Gretel and Baako are huddled together under one blanket beside the horses shielded by a low-branched tree. Our movements cause them both to bolt up, throwing off the blanket.

Baako stands, fists drawn at first, before Gretel runs to Colt. She thrusts her legs around his waist and throws her arms around his neck. "I was so worried."

"You were supposed to go back to the compound." Colt peels his wife off of him and kisses her.

Baako shakes his head. "Have you ever tried to make Gretel do something she didn't want to do?"

"I know what you mean." Colt pats Baako's shoulder. "But we need to hurry."

Tury and the prince ride on one horse and Gretel and the princess ride on Hershey.

Along the way, the mood is somber after we share the news about Miss Brita's fate. We travel only at night. It is slow with the children and only two horses. Thank goodness Baako brought enough food.

All that can be heard is the gentle clapping of the hoofs on the path. When we arrive at Dead Man's ravine, I relax. We're close to Aunt Sandra's place.

"Halt, who goes there?" The voice of the sentry guarding Aunt Sandra's property is the best sound that I have ever heard. We've finally made it. It takes a couple of messages before Aunt Sandra gives the okay for us to enter.

When we exit at the end of the maze, I am surprised that my father, the ambassador, is there to meet us. He picks up the princess first and hugs her, tears streaming down his face. "I have missed you, little girl."

Princess Kamea giggles, "Daddy, mommy was wrong. You did come back!" That makes him cry more.

The ambassador holds up the little prince who he has never seen and studies him. "I'm glad to finally meet you, son."

He cuddles his new son and hugs each of us, me, Riley, Colt, and Baako. "I can't thank you enough. You have brought my life back to me."

Word of the rescue spreads through Aunt Sandra's compound. There is a huge banquet thrown midday with plenty of food and drinks. The mood is festive. Lots of laughs and storytelling. The prince and princess smile and giggle along with everyone else.

I sit by Riley. My cheeks flush being this close to him. I haven't had a chance to talk to him alone. I want to tell him what it means to me that he is back at the compound and safe. I can't seem to stay away from him. Maybe he feels the same way. Maybe he knows how I feel. I don't want to let him go. We don't have to say anything. I just need to be near him.

When he was gone a part of me—the part I love the most was missing. But now—now that we're here together, I am whole again. The food tastes sweeter, the sky seems bluer, and the air smells fresher. Hope is alive in me again.

As the festival winds down, Thomas tells me that Aunt Sandra is searching for Colt and me. Colt hasn't left Gretel's side. Guess they'll be on a perpetual honeymoon all their life. I hope so.

Riley is standing by me when Aunt Sandra approaches. "It's imperative that we keep this positive momentum going. We want you and Colt to address the troops tonight. Tell them what happened. Don't hold anything back. They need some good news. There have been attacks all over and some of the resistance groups have suffered a large number of casualties. We are going to lose the war if we can't win some of the battles. We need you. Will you go on the air for the good of all?"

I glance at Riley. I can't explain it, but I want his approval on my choices. He gives a quick nod and I say to Aunt Sandra, "Of course. I think I can give a very uplifting message tonight."

Colt must have thought the same way since he and Gretel join us as we walk to the radio building.

Inside, Colt and I take our place in front of the microphone. Riley and Gretel sit behind us.

Aunt Sandra pushes the microphone's "on" button and the light flashes on and off. Aunt Sandra says, "Troops of the resistance. I give you Paisley and Colt with their uplifting message on what's going with the resistance front." She looks at Colt.

Colt begins. "We are happy to report that our manufacture of the cure is being amped up and we should be able to deliver as many doses of the cure as the resistance needs in the next two weeks. After that, we will be passing the cure out to all of the people. We will eradicate the virus for good."

He turns the microphone toward me. I take in a deep breath. "There have been more sacrifices by good people. All I can tell you is to hold tight. The cure is on the way. Don't be bullied by the emperor or by his mercenary army. If we stand together, we will win this war."

Colt and I smile at each other and say together, "Power to the resistance."

The lights flash and the set goes dark. Everyone hugs. We are almost at the door to retire to our beds for a good night's sleep when we hear the radio charge back up.

Squawk!

"People of the World."

The voice is that of the emperor. How is he broadcasting over our waves?

I gasp. "Can we make it stop?"

Colt shakes his head. "I don't know how. I don't know how he is transmitting over these airways." His eyes glare with hatred.

I feel my blood boil. What could this maniac, this killer of children, say? It can't be anything good. I take in a big breath as I ready myself for the worst.

"People of the world. Paisley and Colt are nothing but liars and outlaws. They have stolen and lied to you. They have single handedly brought back the virus."

I gasp. Colt squeezes my hand.

"They have used the virus to kill those who oppose them. I have been fortunate enough to escape this, but my wife has not. The queen is on her deathbed, her body ravaged by this deadly virus. My doctors have said she does not have more than a day to live."

I want to make the transmission stop, but I can't. I have to endure the emperor's voice pouring out of the radio speakers. It's difficult to hear about the queen.

The emperor continues his broadcast. "My beautiful and sweet wife is dying because these criminals wanted her dead. I ask you, my admiring public, don't you want someone who will control evil like Paisley and Colt? Do you want them using the virus as a weapon to wipe out all who oppose them?"

"Help me deliver these outlaws, Paisley and Colt, to justice. I want them dead or alive. If you bring them to me, you will live in a palace forever. You will never want for anything. You and your family will have all of the servants you could ever want. You will be treated like kings and queens. You will save your people."

"Bring me Paisley and or Colt and all of these things will be yours."

The radio goes silent.

We all sit for a few moments before Riley breaks the silence. "I don't understand, they didn't even mention me."

The room breaks out in nervous laughter.

It begins.

Chapter 15

When we walk out of the radio station room, most of the inhabitants of the compound are milling about discussing the emperor's words. It's obvious that news of the announcement and its contents has spread. Many people pat Colt and me on the back in a show of support. I can't detect one nonbeliever in the crowd. Wish the rest of the world could know what this group understands. The real truth.

Aunt Sandra shakes my hand. "I have to go now. We will have to double or triple the security. Unfortunately, that announcement might make some good people go bad. He virtually put a target on both of your backs."

Riley shoves in beside me. "You don't have to worry about Paisley. I won't let anything happen to her. "

I am terrified about the possibly of becoming a target and excited about Riley's chivalrous comments all at the same time. Why can't my life be normal?

Aunt Sandra pats Riley's hand. "I know you will do whatever it takes to protect Paisley." She turns to Colt and me. "The resistance and all of its resources will protect you both. This is your haven. We will not let anyone get in here. No one will be able to come near you." Aunt Sandra puts an arm around both mine and Colt's shoulders. "I know that you are sorry that the queen is dying. But there is nothing that you could have done about it."

"I'm not worried about me and Colt." I pull away from Aunt Sandra's hug. "Why did he have some of the virus left anyway?" I cross my arms. "If they didn't have the virus, then they couldn't have injected anyone. It was an easy fix. Why didn't someone make sure all of the virus was destroyed?"

"My fault." My father makes his way up to me, Colt, and Aunt Sandra. "I heard the hacked broadcast. I'm the reason that there was some live virus. I gave him the murder weapon to kill my wife. It seems unreal."

I grab my father's arm. "What would possess you to keep something that dangerous?"

"It's the only way to make an antidote. I had to have some of the live virus. It still took many years of trial and error. I perfected it by using a machine I had invented twelve years ago. The only way that I could have enough science and equipment and money to develop the antidote was to give in to the king." My father covers his face with his hands. "What have I done?"

"You saved the world. Don't ever forget that." I hug him. "You can't blame yourself. I shouldn't have faulted you. You had a perfectly good reason to keep the live virus. I shouldn't have questioned you and your honor. We need you. We needed you to find the cure. If you had not found the cure, then we would still be fearful about the virus."

He shakes his head. "But the cost. Was it worth it?" He looks at both Colt and me. "And now there's a price on your heads and many who will stop at nothing to turn you in. The emperor is blaming you." He buries his head in his hands. "You didn't even know about the virus. How can he do that? I hate that people will believe him."

"You couldn't have known." Aunt Sandra releases Colt and walks over to my father. "You are grieving that the mother of two of your children, is going to die. You are guilt ridden that you made the antidote, but was not able to save your wife."

"I did give it to her while she was pregnant but it didn't work because she grew up with the root that was used as part of the formula that slowed the virus down before the cure was discovered. It changed her metabolism. I could have worked with her blood and developed a cure for just her. But I wasn't given the chance. I didn't give myself the chance because I chose to be selfish. I faked my death and left my wife and my children in the hands of a monster and that monster gave his power over to another more powerful monster and now..."

Aunt Sandra motions for Colt to bring my father a chair. "Sit, ambassador. Think of what you do have. You have brought us the cure. You have Oliver and the prince and princess. You saved many. By giving them the antidote, you saved your children's lives."

A tear runs down my father's cheek. It might be a long time before he can think clearly. Right now, he is riding on the guilt ship and he doesn't seem to be coming to shore anytime soon.

Until we are caught or the emperor gives up on his obsession of finding us, Colt and I might as well be prisoners on Aunt Sandra's safe haven. We can't risk being caught. If we're punished for the outbreak of the virus, the rebels could lose faith. It would endanger our hope of a democracy.

It is not long before the emperor announces, "The Queen is dead." There is a great funeral, with lots of pomp and circumstance. The queen's body is cremated. Fears about the virus possibly returning sweep once again throughout wealthy communities. These people are completely dependent on the emperor for their food and to provide the mercenaries who will fight their war. Because of their dependence, the emperor grows very powerful.

Chatter on the radio is monitored all of the time. People ask every once in a while what has happened to the royal children, Princess Kamea and Prince Ross. Rumors that they are dead circulate, but most of the questioners are answered with a quick change of subject or silence.

The emperor doesn't know what happened to the children. He does know that he gave them an injection of the virus. He likes to spread his favorite rumor that he has the prince and princess safely tucked away in a beautiful countryside villa with constant guards. Elaboration of this rumor include that the children play daily and are happier than they have ever been.

I laugh when I hear these stories because they are close to the truth. The children frolic daily in the meadows of Aunt Sandra's compound. They want for nothing. They have plenty of playmates and a father who adores them and is making up for lost time.

Gretel and the ambassador entrust Colt and Riley to build a replica of the machine in which the cure is synthesized. It's a complicated machine that clones DNA. The cloned DNA used for the cure is mine and the machine being replicated is the one the ambassador designed and built when he was in the Army stationed in Germany before the virus outbreak.

Over the next month, the resistance strengthens, not an easy feat with the emperor feeding the paranoia.

It helps that the vials of cure are distributed worldwide. Oliver begins to reset worldwide communication. There are a few television stations up and running. Every one of the stations is owned by the emperor and the Mercs.

Since airwaves and bands cannot be controlled, Oliver breaks in and broadcasts on one of the stations for the resistance. He calls it "Rogue."

The television stations send out breaking news. Through these communications I find out my friend Ms. DeVane, the original owner of the doll shop that sold the "Sponsored Companions," has been reunited with her son. Oliver guides families back to each other and to the cure. Lieutenant Drake confiscates weapons to arm the resistance fighters all over the globe.

The emperor's propaganda about the reintroduction of the virus does scare many people. Some of our resistance is afraid. We hear rumors of pockets of rebels fleeing the resistance safe havens and seeking refuge with the emperor's side. The wrong side. The emperor and his goons. We do what we can to stop that bleed by reassuring the resistance that we will win the war.

Colt, Riley, and I train the children daily. Despite the conflicting messages from our side and the emperor's side, our numbers are growing. Every day Aunt Sandra's maze brings in new "strays." These strays are children or grown-ups. Usually Undesirables or Uncounteds, but now even a few disgruntled Mercs make their way into the fold. They take the cure and join in training. Lieutenant Drake along with Captain Via have a plan to make sure democracy wins.

Television stations report a date has been set for a meeting and vote by the Consortium of the World, a federation uniting all of the countries of the world. The vote will decide on how our world should be governed. We begin a strong push for democracy on our station messages.

Oliver is on the verge of starting the World Wide Web again. The emperor has been working on this project for a while with no success.

The meeting of the Consortium of the World is to be held in Hamburg because Hamburg is an international port. Many of the countries of the world are able to send dignitaries by ship. All countries must have representation.

The emperor is unaware that my father, the ambassador and author of the first articles proposed by the Consortium of the World and the new father of democracy, is still alive.

Aunt Sandra, Colt, Oliver, Lieutenant Drake, Captain Via, and I plan to attend the meeting. If things start going awry, the ambassador will step in.

I'm hopeful.

If all goes as planned and democracy wins out, then I'll be back on my Ferris wheel farm and harvesting my own food very soon.

A few nights later, Colt and I are waiting for the radio announcement. I check the door. "Where's Aunt Sandra? She's never late to introduce us."

Colt and I patiently wait. "So how's married life, Colt?" I tease, knocking into his shoulder.

"Why? Are you thinking about getting married yourself?"

My cheeks burn and my stomach churns. I squirm in my chair. "What do you mean? I'm not really the marrying kind. I like my independence." I kick his foot.

"Besides, who would I marry?"

"Like you don't know." Colt burst out laughing. "It's so obvious every time you and Riley are together. You know you like him."

A snort escapes my nose. How dignified is that? "I don't know what you're talking about? You know that Riley and I are just friends."

Colt laughs again. "Yeah right, just friends." He leans back in his chair. "So I guess it wouldn't bother you if I told you I saw him talking to that pretty girl Gina."

My face turns hot. My stomach flips a couple of times. "Of course it wouldn't bother me." I don't like Gina. I don't think she's that pretty. How can Colt find her attractive?

The door opens and in walks Gretel. Thank goodness. Gretel is here to stop this ridiculous conversation. Colt doesn't know me at all.

Something's wrong. Gretel's face contorts like she is in pain. I've only seen her like this one other time in my life. It's the same look she made when she saw our mother murdered on live television. I shoot up out of my chair. Something bad has happened. "Gretel, what's wrong?"

"Aunt Sandra just died." Gretel sobs. "Amanda discovered her body." She makes her way to Colt. "Aunt Sandra never woke up from a nap and died peacefully in her sleep."

Gretel cries in Colt's arms as I sit stunned. Aunt Sandra. It can't be.

What will happen to us now?

Chapter 16

The next few days are scattered and unorganized. No one takes charge. Some of the chores get done, while others are neglected. I know that everything will eventually fall apart unless someone takes control. It takes a while for the news to sink in.

Specifics about Aunt Sandra's cause of death are brought to light. Aunt Sandra had been taking medicine to control her diabetes for quite a while. She didn't share her condition with anyone. Why didn't she tell us? We could have been more prepared.

One thing that Aunt Sandra worked out down to the smallest detail is her funeral. Her lists of final wishes keeps everyone busy during a time of great sorrow. I'm happy to have the distraction. The entire compound shuts down for her funeral. Colt and I are to give her eulogy.

In her instructions, Aunt Sandra was very specific that everyone is to gather in the courtyard of the compound. It is a beautiful spot and big enough for all to sit comfortably on the ground or in chairs. The growing flowers and trees will decorate her funeral as they did her life. A fitting setting for her send off. After the funeral, there is to be a great party.

Aunt Sandra left detailed instructions about the food and decorations. A celebration of her life is what she called it. I liked that. Since she lived a large life, it should be celebrated.

That night all of the compound inhabitants pay tribute to Aunt Sandra's life. Because everyone has a part in the celebration, the compound has a purpose and path once again.

A full moon is high in the sky lighting up the night. The air is crisp; not too hot or too cold. It makes me think that Aunt Sandra herself is sitting in heaven directing nature to her specifications. For this one night, there will be no talk of war, democracy, or even viruses. Tonight, we will talk about a great woman. Our Aunt Sandra.

Colt begins the eulogy. "Aunt Sandra chose to live her life to protect others. She gave up her freedom for those quarantined to be free on her farm. Her generosity towards others is legendary. Aunt Sandra will go down in the history books as a friend to the downtrodden and needy." He chokes as he reads his notes.

It's my turn. I take a big breath, determined to get through this with strength. Aunt Sandra would have liked that. "When I first met Aunt Sandra, she could tell that I was telling the truth. She knew my heart. It was a gift and one we will miss terribly. Aunt Sandra fought hard for democracy."

My voice catches for a moment. "She never turned anyone down who needed help. She never recognized a disability; she only saw people's ability. We will miss Aunt Sandra, but we must honor her by carrying on her legacy and fighting for her hope of a new democracy."

I take in another deep breath, fighting the cracking of my voice. "I will fight to my death to make sure that Aunt Sandra's memory lives on. I loved Aunt Sandra."

Tears are shed as others share specific stories. She was such a significant and driving force in the new regime that it's hard to think of going on without her. The children of the compound will especially miss her.

Aunt Sandra was a sounding board for people haunted by problems along with those making hard decisions. But the greatest thing about Aunt Sandra was her ability to tell in a short conversation if a person was good or bad or if his or her intentions were honorable or not. She had become the mother I lost. She took me in when I needed her.

Colt was great at explaining her quirkiness. Her love of that buggy. The way she loved raw potatoes. How she was our best cheerleader on the broadcasts and how she never gave up on freedom.

When the funeral ends, it is time for the dinner. The masses are serene and quiet. I imagine that they are grateful knowing how wonderfully blessed we all were in having Aunt Sandra in our life. Aunt Sandra would be happy to know how much she meant to everyone and how significant her life had been.

Colt announces at the end of the service. "Eat drink and be merry. That was Aunt Sandra's last request for the celebration of her life. It's what she would have wanted."

"That was a nice funeral, Colt. Or I guess I should call it a celebration of life." I touch his arm. "I liked everything you said."

Colt hugs me as Gretel joins him. He and my sister still seem to be one person. I hope they never get over this honeymoon phase. How wonderful to be so much in love. Colt and Gretel join Tury and the little royals, Prince Ross and Princess Kamea.

I am so focused on watching them play a game of stick and ball that I am surprised by Riley when walks up behind me and asks, "What are you doing for the rest of tonight?"

"No plans." I shrug my shoulders. "Not much to do on a night like this. It's time to reflect and think about Aunt Sandra." Thought he would be with Gina tonight. I burn when I think of her. The thought of them together bothers me.

Riley points to the buffet table full of food. "How about we get a plate of food and share more stories about Aunt Sandra?"

The tables are heaped with all different kinds of food. Everyone brings a favorite dish. They raid the food storage to serve a one of a kind meal that will be remembered forever. The aroma of the different food scents is overwhelming in the courtyard. The food looks and smells great. I know that it will most certainly taste as good as it looks.

Colt and Gretel are all curled up with each other and my father is playing with the little royals. Yes, it might be nice to hang out with Riley tonight. It's been forever since we had a real conversation. "Sure. That sounds nice."

Someone has made chicken and dumplings, kielbasa, and a schnitzel. I choose food I don't normally eat.

We take our plates and water over to a nice grassy area. Riley looks at the sky. "Can you believe that moon?"

"Nice spot." I sit down. "I can't believe how full it is." I lean back. "Do you think that Aunt Sandra is smiling down upon us?"

"I'm positive she is." He takes a bite of bread. "Do you remember the first time we met?"

"You mean the first time you tried to turn me in to the Mercs and Hershey knocked you down?" I laugh thinking back to that day. I look at Riley. He has really grown since then. He's taller and more handsome.

Leaning close to me, he touches my neck.

"What are you doing?" I slap at his hand.

He shrinks back. "I just wanted to see if you were still wearing the four-leaf clover?"

"Oh." I pull out the four-leaf clover made from the bullet that was meant to kill Riley. I loved what he said about it. He made something good from something bad. "Yeah, of course I still wear it. You know it's my good luck charm."

"You're my good luck charm." He voice softens and his eyes twinkle in the moonlight.

Riley is the most handsome person I have ever seen. I giggle. "Right. I'm a good luck charm." I twirl the clover in my fingers. "I'm charmed. I've been kidnapped, almost hanged, almost dragged over a ravine, and jumped in a lifeboat..." I stop for a minute.

He leans and nudges my shoulder. "Well if you put it that way."

I wink at him. "I've been on death's bed quite a few times." I toss a grape in my mouth. "I guess none of those times took." I chuckle again.

We burst out laughing. He takes a grape off my plate and throws it at me. "What would the world be like without you in it?"

"Or you." I smile.

Our arms are close, almost touching. He grins. "Do you mean that?"

"Of course I do. I'd miss you if you weren't in my world."

"Good." He lies flat of his back. "I get scared thinking about war. We have to make split second decisions about what we are going to do and when we are going to do it. I don't want to die."

Stretching out on the grass alongside Riley, I prop up on my elbow sideways gazing down at him. "I don't want to die either. I should have died that very first day. If I had been home on the farm and not tried to go and save Colt from the trap then I would have been home when the men raided the farm. They would have discovered that I was there and that I was an Uncounted. What would have happened to me then?"

I suck in air. "Every day since then has been a gift. A beautiful gift where I get to meet people like you and Colt. And Gretel marries my best friend."

"You have a beautiful way of looking at the bright side of life. I love the way you think." He turns his head away for a minute, the back of his neck is beet red.

"I like the way you think too." I slap at his shoulder.

He grabs my wrist to stop me from slapping at him. "And how do I think?"

I rub the four-leaf clover in my fingers. "Take this four-leaf clover for instance. You were almost killed. So what do you do? You make a four-leaf clover. You're an optimist. I like that you can take something bad and make something good out of it."

Smiling, Riley rubs my arm. "How much do you like me?"

"How much do I like you?" Springing upright, I squirm a bit. "I like you just fine." I bump my shoulder into his. "You're one of my best friends."

He sits up for a moment and shoots a wry smile at me. "Best friends huh?" He crosses his arms. "Nothing more?"

"I like you more than other guys." I turn on my side again. "Is it the same as Gretel feels for Colt? I don't know. I don't have time to figure it out. We have the war. To be honest, I don't know how long you or I will survive. Does that answer your question?"

"Yeah it does. I guess I was hoping..." He stops and picks up a blade of grass and throws it.

"Hoping for what?" I stop his arm from leaning over to pick up another piece of grass. "Seriously, hoping for what?"

He shakes his head. "It's stupid after what you just said. I can't tell you now."

"Just tell me."

He takes in a deep breath and comes up on his side so we are facing each other resting our heads on our hands and our elbows on the ground. He says, "I always think today I might die and I don't want to die without ever having kissed a girl." His face turns the most interesting color of crimson. "If I'm going to kiss anybody, I want it to be you, Paisley."

Maybe it's the moment. Maybe it's that he seems so vulnerable. Maybe it's that he wants to kiss me and not Gina. I'm not sure what it is. But right in that moment, I want to kiss him too. He's right. We might die tomorrow.

I take the plunge. "I think my first kiss should be with you too." I close my eyes. I push my face and my lips to his face. He softly leans into my lips. His are moist. It's nice. Nicer than I thought it would be. A quick kiss. Our first kiss. It's sweet. More than sweet, it's magic.

He strokes my face. My stomach jumps and my head squeezes. It's like the feeling I get when I'm riding on my Ferris wheel only a hundred times better. Like I'm falling off the top of the Ferris wheel and I know I'll hit the bottom, but I'm not scared. Heat rises like an electric bolt shooting through the top of my head.

He brushes his hand through my hair. "Thanks. Now I won't die never being kissed."

"Me neither." I take his hand in mine. "But let's try not to die."

We talk about other adventures, about Aunt Sandra, Colt, and Gretel. We gab about everything but that kiss. It almost as if conversing about it would make the kiss disappear.

It's late. I notice most of the party goers have gone to bed.

Riley stands, grabs my hand, and pulls me up. "Guess it's time to go to bed."

"Yeah. I guess so." I turn to grab my plate.

He gets both of our plates, walks toward the garbage cans, scrapes them off, and walks back toward me.

I wave at him. "See you tomorrow."

"Wait a minute." He pulls me near and pauses for a minute, his face close to mine. He leans down and I feel his breath on my lips. His warmth makes me feel safe. He says, "Do you think it would be okay if we had two kisses before we die?'

My eyelids flutter slightly, signaling my permission. He presses his lips to mine and his warm touch is exhilarating, exciting, and scary all at the same time. What is he thinking as his lips caress mine? I am in a trance or something because when he finally releases his embrace, I am almost unable to stand. I don't know what has come over me. I stumble for a minute and he catches me.

"Are you all right?"

I catch my breath. "You?"

He puts his arm around my shoulder. "That was some kiss. Thanks. I can die a happy man now."

"No talk about dying. " I snuggle closer to him. "I say we think about living."

"You're right." He squeezes my shoulder. "You've definitely given me something to live for."

He walks me to my door with a big grin on his face. I peek out the door as he leaves. He is dancing and clicking his heels together. He looks like an idiot.

But as he disappears down the street, I know what he is feeling because I feel it too. My heart is singing out loud.

Chapter 17

It is hard to sleep. My room is glowing from the light of the shining moon. I toss and turn replaying the kiss in my mind. Will it be different between us now? Are we together now? It's hard to know.

I need to talk about this whole night, the kiss, the conversation, everything with Gretel. It's hard to wait until morning to go to the research lab. I am supposed to be training the children. Riley and Colt will wonder where I am. Maybe they'll think I am sleeping in. Good thing Gretel never sleeps late.

As I enter the lab, I'm surprised to see people working. Fires are lit and test tubes are bubbling on every counter in the place. Conversations between technicians make my entrance go unnoticed.

Finally, I spy Gretel holding a clipboard and marking off some kind of a checklist. Always perfectly coiffed–even when we were saving her from the emperor and she had to ride from the ship to the woods, she looked flawless. Must be her skin and hair type. Some people look wonderful all of the time.

She doesn't notice me right off, but my father does. He fiddles with the machine. "Good morning, Paisley," my father says cheerfully. "You look different today. Did you change your hair?"

I pull my hair over my eyes, trying to hide my reddening face, and mumble, "No."

Could my father see that I had been kissed last night? I dismiss the crazy thought and focus my attention to Gretel who is working at the counter.

"They're reading Aunt Sandra's last will and testament publically in the compound square." Gretel jiggles a test tube in her hand and the liquid inside swirls. "Today at noon."

A jolt of reality. I let go of my hair and stand erect. "Where did you hear that?"

My father chimes in. "They announced it at the party." He cuts his eyes over to me. "Where did you go? I was looking for you last night and I couldn't find you anywhere."

I shuffle my feet, spy a rolling office chair, and plop in it. The chair rolls across the floor and I slam into a cabinet. Bam! The chair lunges forward and propels me onto the floor.

A small price to pay to not answer that last question.

"Are you okay?" My father rushes to my side and pulls me up off the floor.

Gretel holds her hand to her mouth trying hard not to burst out laughing. No use. Boisterous chuckles slip through her fingers. I begin giggling, and then my father starts chortling. Gretel attempts to go back to work, but she starts snickering again. Then my father tries returning his attention to his work, but is unsuccessful, letting go of boisterous laughter that fills the room. Technicians whisper and point at us. I can guess the content of their conversations.

I tease. "Ambassador, aren't you supposed to be in charge?"

He snorts as he spits out: "I'm sorry. The image of you flying across the floor was funny." He leans over, his hands rest on his knees, and he coughs from laughing so hard.

The laughing is a nice release from all of the stress. Finally, we're able to regain our composure and my father returns to work on the machine and Gretel fiddles with the test tubes on the counter.

Sliding up next to my sister, I watch as she pours something on a slide and looks through a microscope. "What are you doing?"

"Looking for changes in the virus." She rolls the lens adjuster up and down and writes a notation on paper.

I cock my eyebrows. "Does the virus change?"

"Every virus I have studied has mutated. This particular one hasn't changed since it started which is odd because with its longevity, twelve years, it should have adapted. It's almost as if this is a virus that was manufactured. It hasn't naturally evolved in nature." Gretel pulls the slide out and shakes her head as she studies it.

"I'm not going to try to figure that out. You figure it out. You're the scientist." My fingers drum the counter.

"Don't worry. I will." My sister puts her hand on mine. "Did you want something, Paisley?"

"Why would you think that?" I clasp my hands in my lap. "I just wanted to visit."

"You're supposed to be training the children." She puts the slide down and stares at me. "I'm sensing you came here to talk about something."

My flinch lets her know she is right. I hate that about my sister. She knows me too well. "Yeah, I do need to talk."

Gretel scans the room and sees my father still focused on his machine. A few of the lab assistants are filing in. "Let's go for a walk." She pushes some papers next to the slide. "This can wait." She calls back to my father. "Be back in a minute." He grunts our way.

As we exit the lab door, the morning air is crisp. The hills are glistening with new fallen snow. It's always a little winter here at Aunt Sandra's' place. I miss Aunt Sandra's smiling face. Not many people wandering around. Everyone has a place to be.

Gretel quickens her step. "It's a little colder than I had thought." She pulls the collar of her sweater around her neck. "We must have had a cold front move through last night."

"It was perfect last night." I cross my arms to hug my sweater. I put one arm around my sister's back and rub. "There, better?"

She scrunches in closer to me. "So tell me all about it. I take it this has to do with Riley."

How does she know? Was I that transparent? I mumble a question, "Why would you think that?"

"I saw you two go off together last night and I didn't see you again. That and Riley came by our bungalow this morning to talk to Colt. He dragged him out of bed and everything." She cocks her eyebrow. "What did you do to that boy last night?"

Leaning down and grabbing a bunch of wild flowers, I pluck the petals one at a time. Was Riley upset about last night?

"What did he say?" I toss a petal on the ground.

"I couldn't hear most of it as they went outside, but I heard Paisley this and Paisley that. I think that boy is seriously smitten with you." She places her hands on each of my shoulders. "So spill, what happened?"

"We kissed."

Gretel throws her arms around me. "About time."

I stiffen. "Is that all you have to say?"

"Anything else?" She squeezes me. "Details. Where did it happen?"

Pulling back, I look at her square in the face. "You're not really asking me for details. Are you?"

"Not if you don't want to share." She shrugs her shoulders. "What do you want me to say? Be careful? Wait until you're married? I'm your sister, not your mother. Life is too short. If you have found someone who you like and makes you happy, then I say kiss him some more." She makes a kissing sound smacking her lips. "Kiss him today, kiss him often. Enjoy life. The way things are going, we are not promised tomorrow. Might as well enjoy it while we can." My perfect sister, always knows exactly what to say.

The smile on my face is as big as the smile glowing in my soul. "I will and I might even give you some details at another time when I'm not so embarrassed." I lift my head for a moment and ask, "What time is the reading of Aunt Sandra's will?"

"Noon." My sister hugs me and we stroll back to the lab arm in arm. Usually our talks are of war, human trafficking, slavery, The Undesirables, The Uncounteds, the royals, and the Mercs. Just for today, a new topic to talk about is nice.

At precisely noon, a member of Aunt Sandra's security detail steps into the middle of the square to read Aunt Sandra's last will and testament.

Children and adults line the area. The man uses a bullhorn because of the sheer numbers of people who have gathered. I haven't realized how many people live here now. I crane my neck trying to spot Riley. It will be hard to concentrate on the reading if he is here. Fortunately for me, Colt and I are led up front. We sit among Aunt Sandra's children. No Riley in sight. Better, at least I will listen.

The bullhorn screeches and people cover their ears. Then the officer reads:

"I, Samuel Atkins, was appointed by Sandra Becker, also known as Aunt Sandra and who will be listed as Aunt Sandra from this point forward, to read her last will and testament."

His head is down. He pauses for a moment, swallows hard, and takes a breath.

"Being of sound mind and body, I do hereby bequeath the following: each of my security detail a plot of land predetermined to call their own. My vast lands have been divided. These small plots together equal to five percent of my land. The deeds are registered in the back of this document."

Aunt Sandra didn't leave anything to chance. No wonder she was a great leader.

Mr. Atkins continues reading Aunt Sandra's' last wishes. "If you were on my security detail, then you get a place to call your own. Take care of your families and work the land. I appreciate your service and I hope this small token will somehow repay you for all of the kindness you showed me. I simply say thank you."

Whispers ripple throughout the crowd. Officers shake hands and hug their loved ones.

Mr. Atkins continues, "My one request is that you will consider staying on to protect the next person who runs this compound."

"Who is going to run the compound?" A man shouts from the back. Voices collide as separate speculations and discussions circulate the group.

A loud voice interrupts, "Aunt Sandra's children and grandchildren will inherit the land, that's for sure, but would they run the place also?"

Too many voices for any answers. Mr. Atkins yells for order. Few listen. This will could change everything. What if Aunt Sandra sees fit to divide the compound? Will we be able to still operate this place, the heart of the resistance, without her?

The bullhorn screeches loudly and quiet follows. Mr. Atkins continues, "To my children, grandchildren and one great grandchild, I leave sixty five percent of the rest of my holdings. The following property..."

I gaze off toward the drawbridge. Aunt Sandra's lands are vast and she is generous in her division and precise in where they are located. Still no mention of the thirty percent of her holdings where most of the compound's inhabitants live.

My brain is like cotton. Mr. Atkins's words drone in my head. "West, acres, my beloved..." I quit listening. Standing next to a large tree is Riley.

He first enters from the left side of the crowd. He stops occasionally for a random hand shake or pat on the back. He scans the crowd as he walks. Is he looking for me? It's a few more moments before he spots me. His face lights up. My heart jumps a beat.

Mr. Atkins's voice dissipates as Riley inches his way towards me.

The crowd erupts with loud cheers. The applause is deafening. The crowd hovers closer around me. I lose sight of Riley. Where did he go? I'm hoisted on someone's shoulders. Why are they picking me up?

At this height, I scan the crowd. I spot Riley and I lift my hand to wave to get his attention. He is staring at me and clapping. Another person from the crowd grabs my hand and shakes it.

Totally confused now, I take my focus off Riley and try to listen to Mr. Atkins's words. He is clapping too. The man who holds me on his shoulders takes me to the stage. He sets me down feet first. I stumble for a moment before I see Colt traveling over the crowd on another's shoulders. When he reaches the stage, he is placed beside Mr. Atkins. Gretel is pushed up beside us.

"Power to the resistance!" The crowd shouts. "Power to the resistance! Power to the resistance!"

Colt and I join hands, raising them together over our head in a sign of unity. He smiles and asks through his teeth like a ventriloquist, "Can you believe it?"

"What?" I shake my head at him. "I couldn't hear above all the shouts. What happened? What does the will say?"

Mr. Atkins holds his hands up and shouts above the crowd. "We need to read this last portion again and the rest of the will. Remember this will is Aunt Sandra's last wish."

The crowd quiets and Mr. Atkins continues. "I, Aunt Sandra, owner and ruler of the lands known as Becker Bavaria, do hereby bequeath the following which is the last thirty percent of my land holdings known as the Becker compound and the last portion of my monies: the castle and the compounds, barracks and surrounding lands and 30% of my fortune."

Mr. Atkins looks up from the document and makes eye contact with the crowd. "And rule of the Becker compound is now passed forward to the new leaders." Mr. Atkins takes in a breath. "They own the compound lands free and clear to house the Uncounteds and Undesirables and to grow their own families. The deeds and specifics are listed on the back of this document. Giving this serves as my commitment to the resistance cause and also to ensure the continuation of my legacy. The compound is given in equal portions to Paisley Mueller and Colt Granger."

Loud cheers erupt.

Mr. Atkins pumps his hands palms down to quiet the crowd. "Be patient. Just a bit more."

"Shhh." The crowd whispers.

"Paisley and Colt have been an inspiration to us all. I ask that you follow their lead as you have always followed mine. To my children and heirs, I have amassed a fortune and have seen fit to break off part of it to continue my legacy. I know this will free you to pursue your own happiness without the burden of continuing my legacy. I love you, all of my heirs."

"Paisley and Colt, I entrust our cause to you along with the future of the world. I have every belief that you two will see it to the end. You have no idea how peaceful my end will be, knowing that my work will be in such loving hands."

"Power to the Resistance. Carry on my family born to me and the family I have chosen and who has chosen me. I love you all."

Mr. Atkins folds the document in his hands.

Aunt Sandra's family joins Colt and me by joining their hands with ours. One of Aunt Sandra's daughters hugs my sister and me and whispers in our ears. "She called all of us in and told us what she had planned. We all agreed with her. It was a family decision to leave you and Colt with the running of the compound. None of us has the inclination, drive, or knowledge and it was so important to her. I know she is smiling down upon us today."

A tear runs down my cheek. I'm overwhelmed. I feel an arm around my waist and I am swooped up into a massive embrace. The smell is familiar and enticing. It's Riley. I whisper to him, my lips almost touching his ear. "I was looking for you."

He breathes into my ear. "Our time will come later. You are one of the leaders of the revolution." He pulls back and gazes into my eyes. "I would follow you anywhere."

Chapter 18

The next few minutes are a blur. It's hard not being able to talk to Riley alone, but I have a feeling that's the way it's going to be for a while.

After the announcement, Mr. Atkins points to a bearded man and says, "Follow him to the house. He will show you around." Colt and I accompany the bearded man to Aunt Sandra's house on the compound. It's located in the main castle.

The bearded man extends his hand to me. "I thought I should formally introduce myself. It was a little crazy this afternoon. I'm Mark. I've overseen Aunt Sandra's properties for years. You own a portion of those properties so I hope you will keep me on, at least through the transition."

I shake his hand. "Transition?"

When I release Mark's hand, Colt grabs it with both of his and gives it a vigorous shake which almost causes Mark to fall down. "Of course you'll stay on. Paisley and I need help. We train children and speak on the radio; we are clueless about all of this. This was a total surprise."

What is Colt saying? He is making us sound like we are total idiots. I know I am not an idiot. "We catch on fast, Mark, but of course we want you to stay on and we would love any help that you have to offer."

Mark opens a door to an outside one-room bungalow that sits adjacent to the castle. I peek in to the sparsely decorated room. A chair and a small bed and a counter are all that are housed in the small abode.

"Since you said you want me to stay on, these are my quarters and if it's okay with both of you, I will stay out here. I can be in the main house in a matter of seconds." Mark bends his head slightly first to me and then to Colt. "It will be an honor to serve the leaders of the revolution."

His room is lovely albeit sparse. It is very utilitarian. I wonder if the castle will be this way.

As Mark walks us toward the castle, I can't contain my excitement at being able to tour Aunt Sandra's house. Sitting down in my dwelling, I often wondered what was inside Aunt Sandra's living quarters. I had never been invited in this inner sanctum.

As I enter the castle, it is just as I expected. Several antiques fill the space. It is ornate, but in a medieval way. The wood mantel above the fireplace is large and imperfect, but fitting for the residence.

Boxes are scattered about with frames and pictures. I assume that the security and family are boxing up Aunt Sandra's personal effects. The walls are stone. Castles back in the day were built to withstand war. A good thing, since our largest battles are still to come.

Mark opens another door. It opens into a large bedroom. "I didn't know which room each of you would want. I guessed Paisley would take Aunt Sandra's old bedroom. We're in the process of packing up her things for her children. We're switching out her furniture to some in storage." He stops for a moment and looks at us. "Aunt Sandra left specific instructions about the items that would go to her children."

"Of course," I stammer. "Whatever she wanted." I freeze for a minute and glance toward Mark. "Wait, are we supposed to move into the castle?"

Mark cocks an eyebrow. "I thought you understood that at the reading of the will."

"Wait a minute." Colt holds up his hands. "I don't know about moving. I mean Paisley can move in here because it's just her, but I want to live with my wife."

"Of course." The corners of Mark's lips turn upward slightly. "No reason to get upset. Calm down."

"What about Gretel?" Colt frowns.

"I'll have a security officer pick up your wife now." Mark leaves for a moment.

After Mark exits, I stare at Colt. "I don't know how to react to all of this. Do you think we can do everything that Aunt Sandra did?"

"Absolutely not!" Colt shakes his head. "But we have to try."

"You're right." I take in a deep breath. "It's what she wanted and she was a wise woman." A tear runs down my cheek.

Mark returns. "Gretel will be here in a moment. I figure she might be the one to pick which area you will live in. There are many choices. Many of them better for a growing family."

Colt's cheeks redden. "Okay, I'll wait on her to decide the room or if we will move in here. I will do whatever she wants."

"The castle is much more convenient. She might want to convert one of the rooms into a personal workshop." Mark guides us deeper into Aunt Sandra's room. "Ultimately, it's your choice, but I think that Paisley should take this room. It has a balcony, the personal radio station..."

"A personal radio station?" I walk over to the table and look over the microphone and the board similar to the one in the radio station. "I didn't realize that Aunt Sandra could communicate on her own."

Mark picks up a microphone and sets it back down. "There are many things that you don't know. That's why I am here. I am going to walk you and Colt and of course Gretel through all of the secrets of the Becker Bavarian Castle."

A knock at the door alerts us to another man. "I have Miss Gretel."

"Mrs." Colt corrects.

The man stammer. "Of course, Mrs. Gretel."

Gretel walks into the room beside Colt. "Well, the missus is here. What's all of this about? They drag me out of my lab right in the middle of an experiment. My work is important too."

Colt holds his finger to his wife's lips. "They want us to live here. They say that you can have your own personal lab. You can conduct all of the experiments you want at all hours of the night without ever leaving home."

"Really? My own personal lab. I like the sound of that." Gretel looks around Aunt Sandra's room. "In here? I don't see any place I could set up a lab in here."

Mark interrupts her. "You arrived quicker than I thought you would. We were just establishing Paisley would be staying in here." Mark looks at me. "Right, Paisley?" I dip my head slightly and he continues, "There is security around the clock, the personal radio, your own bathroom, dressing area, and ..." he opens another door to a sitting room.

Inside is a large conference table with chairs all around. Bookshelves full of books line all three walls. File cabinets take up the back wall. There are no windows. There is a large map spread out on the table with troop's movements and marks indicating resistance group's locations.

I run my fingers across the map. "Is this a war room?"

Mark scans the area. "Aunt Sandra never named it. But war room seems appropriate. Her heirs will not be taking anything out of here. This is all of the information we have gathered about the resistance." He pulls a book off the shelf. "We have a list of all of the people we have identified as resistance fighters." He hands the book over to me.

I open to a page. "There's a lot in here." Written in the ledger complete with headings are names and locations, along with a paragraph or two about each individual's personal journey during the twelve years of quarantine and after. "How did you get all of this information?"

"It took years." Mark takes the book, rubs the cover with reverence, and replaces it back on the shelf. He points to the computer. "We have it all stored on there now."

"Where did you get that?" I run my finger over the keyboard.

"Oliver Grayson." Mark mentions my brother's name without any fanfare. My brother, one of the main reasons we might win this war. My chest juts out slightly. It makes me proud that he's my brother.

"He is on the verge of reestablishing the World Wide Web and through him, we have been able to construct computers from components with his direction." Mark flips to a clipboard page with a diagram. "It's a much more efficient way to communicate and keep data." He sighs. "Although Aunt Sandra's way definitely did have its charm." He murmured Aunt Sandra's name with a respectful tone. We all respected Aunt Sandra. She will be missed.

Colt pipes in. "Yeah, this will be where Paisley stays." He taps my forehead. "Somebody had to make the decision."

I'm sad about the reason, but I have to admit I'm a little excited to have this much power. I had no idea that Aunt Sandra was this involved. Is there more I don't know about?

Mark leads us out. "Paisley, your room will be ready tomorrow night. I'll have one of your security detail come and help you pack tonight."

"That won't be necessary. I don't have much. I can get it all just fine. I might need help tomorrow morning bringing it here. So it will be okay to send someone tomorrow morning."

"Let's go find our new living quarters." Colt tickles Gretel's side and she laughs.

Mark, Gretel, Colt, and I tour the rest of the house. Colt and Gretel decide on three adjoining rooms on the other wing of the castle. As Colt says, "Far enough away from the sister-in-law to have some private time." Gretel and I both turn red.

Their three-room wing will house their bedroom, Gretel's personal lab and a personal communication and war room for Colt.

Gretel asks, "What about the ambassador? Could he move in too?" She looks at me. "It would be so much easier to develop the cure if we were both here."

Colt agrees.

Mark shrugs, "That's entirely up to Paisley and Colt."

"Yes." I feel my face light up. I'm excited to think about my family living under the same roof. "I think that is a great idea and it would be safer for Prince Ross and Princess Kamea with all of this security. We probably need to find a place for Tury too. Tury has been the royal children's babysitter since they escaped the ship."

Gretel weaves her arm through Colt's crooked elbow. "Colt, let's go and get our stuff. I want to set up the lab tonight." She turns to me. "Would you like for us to tell the ambassador?"

"Definitely." I might not be able to control my emotions telling my own father that I want him to move in with me. Gretel could use the lab as the reason. Yes, that would work for me.

"Guess we're not training the children today?" Colt asks as he opens the outside door.

I turn to take a last look at the inside of the castle. Can't believe I'm going to live here. "I'll drop by and put Thomas and Mike in charge. Training needs to continue, but we might not be there as much as we used to be."

Colt waits for Gretel to exit in front of him. "That's true, tell them we'll be available to consult or for emergencies but not much else." Colt turns his attention back to Gretel and slips his arm around her waist and gazes into her eyes. "We going to pack so we can move in tonight."

Dipping my head to indicate my understanding, I rush out in front of Colt and Gretel, looking for the one person I want to talk to. Riley.

Unfortunately, I run into Mike first. "Colt, Gretel and I are moving into the castle to run things. You and Thomas are going to have to continue the training."

"I'll tell Thomas. I think we are ready." Mike puffs his chest out.

"We'll come as much as we can, but it might not be as much as before."

"Thomas and I can handle it." He touches my arm. "You and Colt have trained us well. We're ready to take over. You're needed elsewhere. Aunt Sandra believed in you and Colt and I do too." He leaves, heading to the training area.

As I turn toward the workshop, I see Gretel and Colt exiting the lab with my father trailing behind. He smiles at me and I know that he has been given the

181

news. The prince and princess will be told next since Colt and Gretel are making the move today. Where's Riley? I'm desperate to find him. I want to be the one to tell him.

I dash to his bungalow, but he is nowhere in sight. I check his favorite eating area. He's not here. I look everywhere I can think of, but no Riley. Where is he?

Finally, I walk over to the place on the northwest quadrant where we kissed for the first time and there he sits. Alone, his head rests on his knees. When he hears my movement, he faces me. He's not happy, the corners of his mouth and eyes are curled downward. He looks sad and dejected. Is it because of me?

"You okay?" I slide in beside him and crook my arm in his. He slumps. I can tell by the limpness of his frame that he has heard the news. "I tried to find you. I wanted to tell you first. It came as a complete surprise."

He squeezes my hand. "It's the best choice. I know *that* in my head. I heard you were looking for me. I know you tried to tell me first." His eyes hold a sadness that breaks my heart.

"Who told you?"

"Colt."

That makes me feel better. I'm glad it wasn't some random person. "Then why so sad?"

"He told me about the security." He brushes my hair with his hand. "We won't be able to see each other like this for a long time. Probably not until after the war."

Leaning up close so I can inhale him, I pull his face to mine. "Then we better make the most of it."

He turns his body to face me, places his hand behind my head, and wraps his other arm around my waist. I melt into him and we embrace. I bury my head in his shoulder and he kisses the back of my head. He whispers. "It'll be hard to not be able to hold you this way."

"I'm not in jail."

His lips caress mine ever so lightly. I want to stay like this forever. I want to forget about the war, the Undesirables, and the Uncounteds. I just want to run away with Riley. We could kiss and hold each other until the end of time. I love his kiss, his touch, and the way he holds my head and rubs my back. Time stops when I am in Riley's arms.

My face flushes and I feel faint. "Wait."

"Are you okay?" He immediately stops and faces me. "Do you want me to stop?"

"I'm sorry." I rub my head. "I just got hot all of a sudden. I thought I was going to faint."

He hugs me close. "I feel it too. It's like I have all of these emotions and when I look at you I'm whole, but when I touch you or kiss you all of this passion arises like it's sitting on top of my skin shouting. My heart, so empty before, overflows, erupting each time I'm near you."

"How are you able to verbalize my emotions?" I choke back the tears. "It's amazing. I could never say exactly what I'm feeling."

"We're in harmony." He rubs my hair again ever so lightly. "It's like we're playing the exact same song."

My eyes brim. I can't speak. I'm trembling. "How can you be so perfect?"

"I'm not perfect." He laughs. "Far from it." He kisses the top of my head. "And you. You can say what you feel. You do it every time you speak to the troops. You give me the courage to fight. I'm not afraid. You make us all want to be the very best that we can be. You're wonderful. I'm so happy that you are here and in my life."

He leans in and kisses me again, lightly, and sweetly. "Go live in your castle. I will wait for you forever and a day."

A tear runs down my cheek. I never want to leave.

Hrumph!

A sound comes from behind us. Riley and I release our embrace. I trip trying to stand up. Riley grabs my arm as I straighten my clothes trying to pretend that this stranger didn't see anything embarrassing.

"Hello. I'm Darrell. Your personal bodyguard. Sorry about the intrusion, Miss Paisley. The whole camp has been looking for you. Now that you are our new leader, you must be protected at all times. I pledge that I will give my life for you." He salutes.

I snap my hand to my forehead. "Just Paisley is good enough."

Riley whispers, "Maybe you *are* in jail."

The red in my face begins to subside and I chuckle. This is what my life will be like until the war is over. I am so thankful for my last moments alone with Riley. Now that I have him, my thirst for a normal life is more than it has ever been. I have a taste of freedom. Freedom to kiss, to love, to see who you want. That kind of life is worth fighting for.

We steal a last glance before we separate. Riley leans his lips close to my ear and whispers, "I'm glad to know you will be safe. Until next time."

I touch Riley's hands slightly before leaving him, silently pledging to win this war for me, for Riley, for us all.

Chapter 19

Settling into my role as leader is an easier transition than I thought it would be, possibly because everyone is helping me. There's a revolving door of well-wishers catching me up on how things were done, making suggestions regarding how they think things can improve, and providing nonstop assistance.

Everyone wants me to succeed and they will do just about anything to make that happen. They explain codes, decipher books, suggest varying combat scenarios, or anything else they feel will help. With all of the support, it doesn't take long for me to move into my new room and orient myself to the war room and to the computer.

After a couple of nights, I decide to try the radio. I flip on the switch and lights flash on and off. "PACO here."

The microphone squawks and Oliver's voice rings out. ""This is not PACO. The radio sign and location do not match. Could this be another call sign?"

Is Oliver trying to get me to identify Aunt Sandra's sign? I look around the table and don't see anything that could possibly be a call sign.

I press the button. "I will get back to you on that call sign."

Oliver's voice booms out. "Initials?"

He knows what the call sign is. Why is he making me search for it? I look at the top of the door on the inside. Each door has a big BBF blazoned on the top. Becker Bavarian Farm.

I press the button again. "BBF here."

A noise. A beep, then a voice. "This is SONOL, come in BBF."

"Hey, I guess I figured out what the call sign is. What's going on?"

The light flashes. "We're glad that you are on line again. We're sorry to hear about our loss. We need another broadcast tonight by our two favorite people.

A secret message will be coming shortly. It will only be broadcast on this BFF channel, but it needs to be rebroadcast from PACO. You will need to write it down exactly. It's a message for the troops. Do you understand?"

"Yes." I speak into the microphone and hold my breath waiting for the message. It comes too quickly. I don't have a chance to get anything to write on or write with. A voice I don't recognize says: "Emergency message. Please take this down. Joy is imminent in SA number five, C number 3, NA number 10, and E number 3—heads up about that one BBF. We need our two favorite people to tell factions that the only safe food to eat today is the noodle, the egg, spinach and walnuts are not good eating today. Be aware. Don't get compromised."

I beep in again. "What are you saying?"

"BBF, write this down. It's an emergency. Please get the message out immediately."

Grabbing a notebook and picking up a pen. I beep in again. "Okay I have a pen. Please repeat."

"Joy is imminent in SA number five, C number 3, NA number 10, and E number 3—heads up about that one BBF. We need our two favorite people to tell factions that the only safe food to eat today is the noodle. The egg, spinach and walnuts are not good eating today. Be aware. Don't get compromised."

"Emergency message terminated." The lights cease to flash.

A long sigh escapes my lungs, my shoulders droop. "What in the world?"

"Paisley?" A voice startles me.

"Colt." I stand up, fists raised. "Don't sneak up on me. You scared the life out of me." I lower my fists and show him the paper. "Thank goodness you're here. I need help. Colt, Oliver sent us a message. We need to decipher it and send it out."

Colt pulls up a chair and grabs the paper out of my hand "What do the initials mean? A name? A place? Who's in charge?"

I shake my head. "I don't know. Let's look in some of the books. I have no idea how to decode this message. Maybe Aunt Sandra left a clue somewhere."

We flip through pages of different books. I try to see if anything falls out. Colt studies the table of contents. "Nothing here."

Reading the spines of the notebooks is no help. Nothing anywhere near the codes that are on the message. "We have to go on air in less than thirty minutes. How could Aunt Sandra have trusted us? We're messing up already and we haven't even moved in yet. We are going to lose the war and it's going to be our fault." I sit on the floor in the middle of the strewn books and put my face in my hands.

Books clap open and closed as Colt searches through them. Each time he drops one to the floor, he lets out a big sigh signaling growing frustration with each failure. "Maybe if we had a map. Is there a map of where the troops are and the resistance is located?" He rubs the back of his neck as beads of sweat form around his temple.

"Look!" I peek through my fingers at the map sitting on the table. "Initials." I sprint to my feet. The number "3" stares at me. "Wait a minute."

Colt sees it at the same time I do. "The initials are continents. SA is South America."

I point above it. "NA is North America."

He finishes the initials. "C is Canada. E is Europe."

Making my way around to his side of the map, I see it's South America. What does the number "5" have to do with South America? What are these?" A series of stickpins identify various locations.

Colt pulls a set apart. "This one has four. Are there any in South America that have five pins?"

"Five?" I scan the continent. "Yes, this one has five."

Colt is meticulous. He counts the pins two times each making sure that none of the groupings has five. "No, so where are the pins with five? What's that location?"

"Argentina." I point to the numbers. It makes sense now. "Number the countries in South America, one is Columbia, two is Brazil, three is Paraguay, four is Uruguay, and five is Argentina. Argentina is going to be attacked!"

Colt looks at the clock. "We have to hurry. We're now down to twenty minutes until we have to broadcast."

"Quit talking and count." I examine the amount of pins. "Concentrate on Canada. Less pins."

"Only four. So one is British Columbia, two is Manitoba, three is Ontario. So Ontario is the one that we need to worry about," Colt gasps. "They are being attacked tonight."

I scream, "Hurry! Time is running out!"

He moves around the map to North America. "This country has so many."

I say, "Just pick one and count it. Look at Florida. I'm interested in Florida. It's the only place in North America that I've ever been to. I loved it there."

"How did you know? Florida has ten pins." Colt looks up.

"Lucky guess," I say, "So Florida is being attacked tonight. Only one left. Europe."

Colt looks at the left side. "Fewer pins on the left side. Start counting."

Our home has to be counted. I shake my head. "Count Germany."

"Three." Colt turns ashen. "It's us."

Colt flashes a side view to the clock. "Ten minutes! What's the rest of the message?"

Picking up the note, I read. "Eggs, noodles, spinach and walnuts. What could that possibly mean?"

Colt shakes his head. "I have no idea. Five minutes left."

"Get to the radio." I take a deep breath. "Start the broadcast and give them the first part of the message and I'll try to figure out what the end means. Maybe they'll understand. I hope so."

Jerking up the paper, Colt bolts out the door. "I hope I make it in time. Come as soon as you can."

I start pulling books off the shelf, looking at spines. No book on cooking or foods or anything like that. Eggs, Noodles, Spinach and Walnuts. I keep repeating the same four words. What does it mean? I'm breathing hard. I shut my eyes trying to calm my heart down. It's beating out of my chest. I jerk a piece of paper in front of me, grab a pen, and write the words down

Eggs

Noodles

Spinach

Walnuts

Try first letters, maybe they mean something. Maybe that is the clue.

Eggs

Noodles

Spinach

Walnuts

E,N,S,W. "OooHHH!" East, North, South, and West. I look at the supply areas for each faction. There is an east, a south, a north, and a west distribution center. This is where they will stock up on guns, weapons, everything they need. Oh no, they must be watching all of the supply areas except noodle or the north. My feet clomp on the hardwood floors as I dash out of the house, almost knocking a vase off a table at the front door. My poor bodyguard goes crazy when I sprint out toward the radio building. "Sorry, Darrell. I have to hurry."

He yells back, "Right behind you."

Slinging the door open, I pant for air as I hear Colt giving the directions. He has just finished. "...aware. Don't get compromised."

"Wait." I jump in. "Important. JOY is coming to SA number five, C number 3, NA number 10, and E number 3—heads up about that one BBF. The egg, spinach, and walnuts are no good today only thing safe to eat is the noodles. Make sure you eat the noodles."

I grab Colt's arm and raise both of our hands in the air. "Power to the resistance. Over and Out."

The power shuts down and the lights go dark.

Colt shakes his head. "You realize that they can't see us holding up our hands. We just do that when they see us."

"I like doing it." I turn my chair to face him. "I found out what the message meant."

"No kidding." Colt crosses his arms. "I'm not sure what gave it away. That you ran in here like a crazy person or that you emphasized everything in the message. I think they got it Paisley. So fill me in. What does it mean?"

"We were right about the continents and everything but the eggs, noodle, and all of that is directions." I pull out the paper. "Noodle is north so the supply station to the north is the only safe one in which to get guns and replenish supplies. I take it the others have been compromised or raided or are being watched. Either way, it is not safe for them to go. Joy is a military term for snipers. No joy means it is not clear and joy means there is a clear shot. So in this case joy means that these resistance stations are going to be hit tonight."

Colt takes a deep breath. "What can we do?"

"I don't know. Should we call Oliver and contact Lieutenant Drake or Captain Via and see if we can offer any help from here?"

Colt swings his arms around to the microphone. "It couldn't hurt." The radio hums. "PACO to SONOL."

"SONOL here. That was quite a message tonight."

Pressing the button again, I speak. "Sorry. My fault I got a little carried away."

SONOL comes back. "Yes. E three had already sent a convoy to get the package of spinach. They may be in trouble."

Southern Germany is close to us. "Near here." I speak into the microphone.

"Be careful. Radio silence until tomorrow 1530. Good luck SONOL over and out."

My eyes lock with Colt's. "The ravine and the cave. It's right on top of my farm. We have to go help them."

Colt's eyes look up to the ceiling. "We can't send out the children. They're not ready. We could deploy a small convoy to intercept. Wouldn't need more than four."

As I spring to my feet, heat rises in my face. "I know what you are thinking—you and three more. You're taking me. I'm coming. You are not leaving me behind."

Colt grabs my shoulders. "We can't risk us both."

I grasp his hand. "We know that area the best. The back roads—we can find them when no one else can. You know the caves." I raise our arms over our head. "Together we stand."

"You're right." Colt drops his arm, releasing mine. "We can go and get back before anyone misses us. You and me. Who else?"

"My bodyguard. I won't be able to get away from him anyway."

"There is one other person who knows the lay of the land." Colt pulls on his backpack. "Riley."

Chapter 20

Colt opens the door. Rain pelts down and he pulls his jacket over his head. "I'll find Riley. You tell your bodyguard. We'll meet you at the maze."

I step outside, holding my arm over my eyes to shield the raindrops. "Do we need weapons?"

"Not you." He bops me on the head. "Riley, Darrell, and I will be packing. Not you."

He's probably right. I don't know if I could shoot anyone. I am excited to be able to spend time with Riley and ride my horse, Hershey. Now if we can just make sure we save the group before they are in danger. This rain and a muddy trail will slow us down.

Bodyguards are not allowed to question orders so Darrell is easy. Colt and I made our own choice to go on this mission. No one has jurisdiction over us to talk us out of it or tell us we can't leave. It's a lot of power and responsibility.

Darrell and I enter the maze. We are saluted at each sentry post, but not questioned. At the end of the maze, Riley and Colt stand ready.

Riley holds onto Hershey's reins. "Wasn't a question about which horse you would ride."

Smiling as he gives me a leg up to mount my horse, I enjoy Riley's warm touch. I murmur, "Thanks." My clothes, wet from the rain, adhere to my body. It takes a moment to shift my shirt into the right place.

"Stick by me." Riley mounts his horse and shakes his head, spraying raindrops everywhere.

I flick Hershey's reins and the horse canters to the front through the drizzling rain. "I'm now the boss."

Riley rides next to me. "I told Colt I didn't think you should come, but he reminded me that you two are in charge. It's not that I don't think you can do it. It's that I don't want you to get hurt."

"I understand." I pull out the four-leaf clover. "That's what this is for."

Staring at the necklace, he grins. Darrell and Colt hang back. It is not lost on me that Riley talked to Colt so he knows about us. Darrell caught us kissing so in reality this is a trip where Riley and I don't have to pretend. That makes it nice. I reach over and clasp his hand. I'm glad we can have this time.

Riley squeezes my hand. No looking back at the others. He never pretends. What you see is what you get. It's one of the things I love about Riley. Do I love Riley? What a time to wonder about that. We're on our way to confront a Merc posse.

Muddy trails and the pelting rain slow us, but also hide our movements. We follow the familiar path using short cuts here and there and before long, we hear talking.

"Shush!" Colt whispers. We communicate through hand signals. First, we slip off the horses and each one hands me their horse's reins. I hold the horses to free the guys to cock and ready their weapons. They move forward toward the voices.

Don't panic, I remind myself as I nuzzle Hershey, running my fingers over his wet coat. I try not to imagine what is happening with Riley, Colt, and Darrell.

Waiting is horrible. I squat beside Hershey. What are they doing?

"Paisley? Paisley?" Riley's voice sounds through the rain. "Where are you?"

I lead Hershey toward Riley's voice and see the others. "What happened? Did you find them? Did you warn them?"

"Yes." Colt takes off his jacket and wrings it out before he pulls it back on. "We sent them home, but something seems off. There was no sign of an invasion. I have a bad feeling. We need to get back to the compound."

Riley grabs me around the waist and lifts me on Hershey. "Colt's right. This could be a set up."

"I agree." I squeeze my legs into Hershey's sides and turn toward home. The four of us waste no time trotting back. The rain has slowed, but the terrain is muddy. The sun is coming up as we see the edge of our haven. We tie the horses up and rush back through the maze.

At the end of the maze, we are saluted by the guards. I quickly return the salute. "Let's go to the radio house and see what if anything happened last night."

We pass muddy paths in between the various stone living quarters. The weather keeps the inhabitants inside and off of the streets. I'm happy there is no one to stop us or slow us down. Inside the radio room, Thomas is acting as a radio operator with a long pad full of writing.

"That's a lot of notes." I observe. "What happened?"

"Got word there is supposed to be another announcement." Thomas hands me the list with messages scrawled in the margins. "I looked all over for you. I didn't know what to do so I decided to stay and transcribe the chatter. Where were you?"

"What does it say?" Colt takes the list from my hand. "How about Gretel? Did Gretel realize you couldn't find me?"

"Yes." Thomas stares at him. "She was crying."

"I need to find her." Colt hands the list back to me. "She's probably out of her mind with worry. Let me know what you find out."

"Go." I shove my hand toward him. "Riley and I will figure this out and stay for the message." I look back at Riley, who nods. I knew I could count on him.

Colt bolts out the door.

Darrell walks toward the exit. "Don't leave this room. I'll wait for you outside." He looks at Riley. "I'll be right outside the door. She is not allowed to walk without escort."

Riley nods. "Don't worry she's not going anywhere without you." Darrell's chest puffs out as he closes the outside door behind him.

Thomas stands and pulls on his jacket. "Let me know if you need me to man the radio again. I'm heading home to get some sleep."

"Thanks for staying." I follow him to the door. "When is the announcement supposed to come?"

"It won't be long now." Thomas disappears out of the door.

It isn't two minutes before the lights flash on the radio.

No introduction of the SONOL or PACO. I don't recognize any call signs and the setup is all wrong.

The voice. It's the emperor. "This is your emperor speaking. You have been listening to this fanatical radio broadcast for months. I am here to tell you that the radical radio station has finally been found in a suburb in Hamburg. The culprits were arrested. Lieutenant Drake is in custody. He's been a menace to the government, fraudulently calling himself a lieutenant."

I spring up and fall into Riley's arms. "They've hacked our radio broadcast. Was this all a ruse to get us to be off guard? Or what?"

Riley sets me down gently into the chair. "We need to listen."

Sniffing as I wipe tears from my cheek, I sit up. "You're right."

"Captain Via has also been captured."

I gasp.

"Captain Via saw fit to travel from America to Europe to go against the Consortium of the World. The last arrest is a very upsetting one to tell you about, my fellow world inhabitants. I know that you all loved Ambassador Grayson. He and my wife, the late queen, and her father the great King Ahomana, saved us during the terrible virus outbreak. None of us will ever forget the day the king brought the root to us that staved off the virus. And all of the years our beloved ambassador worked on the cure. "

I'm going to vomit! What a liar! My blood boils. I am enraged. The emperor killed the king and conspired to kill the ambassador. Would people believe him? I don't want to, but I know I have to focus and listen to this evil. I squeeze Riley's hand.

"People of the world, the last of the leaders of this heinous group is none other than Oliver Grayson, son of our beloved ambassador. It seems that he has been rebelling against the government, the mercenary army put in place to keep order, and the royals themselves. The royals are his family. Oliver is a royal. Lieutenant Drake and Captain Via will be tried for their crimes of treason and treachery. If found guilty, they will be put to death."

"Our sweet Oliver, who has been led astray by these hooligans, will not be harmed in any way. We will keep him in the bosom of our government and make sure that he is rehabilitated. We want what is best for the citizens. We will stick together and drive out this underground force. Emperor Richard signing off."

The microphone squawks one last time and the light on the board flashes off.

Colt rushes in with Gretel. It takes Riley and me a few minutes to fill them in.

"What are we going to do?" I ask, hugging my sister.

Colt sits in one of the straight back chairs. "We'll think of something. We always do."

Just then, there is another squawk from the radio. A menacingly evil, familiar voice is speaking. "Paisley and Colt, I know you can hear me."

I drop into a chair beside Colt.

"I know that you monitor this channel and that you are behind the resistance. I am a peaceful man looking for peaceful solutions. Turn yourselves in."

Colt whispers under his breath. "Never."

"Trade yourselves and I will let all traitors go. Lieutenant Drake, Captain Via, and all of these little Undesirable and Uncounted children you love so much. You will get a fair trial in front of the Consortium of the World. It meets in one week. Please come and be heard, and let others ask you questions. Answer for the crimes which you are accused of. The whole world is listening. I'm calling you out. Come and face your judge and jury. If you are found not guilty, all will be released."

"Liar." Gretel murmurs.

"If you are found guilty, you two will be the only ones put to death. You can save all of your people. You have until next Sunday at 1200. We will all be at the Consortium of the World in Hamburg. Save your people. Face your peers. Signing off, Emperor Richard"

My eyes look deeply into Colt's.

His sweaty hand squeezes mine.

We know what we must do.

Make sure both of us, Colt and I, are in Hamburg in a week.

We have to try to save them.

Chapter 21

"**N**o! I know what you're thinking." Gretel swings her arms around Colt. "You can't leave me. I love you. Don't listen to him. Find another way."

Colt embraces his sobbing wife. "I'm not going anywhere tonight." He looks back at me. "We'll talk tomorrow. I'm going to take Gretel home." He picks her up and carries her out the door.

Riley and I sit quietly alone. I don't want to leave. I place my hand on Riley's cheek. "I have no choice. I have to try. You do know that, don't you?"

His eyes fall. "I don't know anything of the sort. We'll find something else to trade. Anything else." He leans in, holds the back of my head, and presses his cheek to mine. "I would give my life for yours without hesitation." He whispers. "You know that."

I grab both sides of his head. "And that is exactly why you must understand why I'm willing to give my life for so many. It's a fair trade."

He pulls my lips to within an inch of his. "There is nothing fair about it."

Darrell peeks in. "Miss Paisley."

Riley lets go of my head.

"I'm right out here if you need me."

"Thanks Darrell. Everything is fine. I'll be out in a minute." I cock an eyebrow at Riley.

"Don't go." Riley leans back in his chair. "Stay. It makes me crazy to think about losing you. I can't imagine life without you."

I stand up, walk over, sit in his lap, and cuddle with him, my head on his shoulder. "I'll have to present and defend my side of the story before the Consortium of the World. I have to answer for how I have conducted myself. If we produce enough evidence, we can end the emperor's tyrannical reign and stop this war. We can bring democracy back. Isn't that worth the risk?"

"Maybe I'm being selfish, but no it's not." His lips caress mine. He rubs my back and my arms. He takes in a deep breath. "I love the way you smell." He leans over and rubs his lips along the nape of my neck. "I love the way you feel." He grabs the small of my back, presses me up close to him, and kisses me again. "I love the way you taste. I can't lose you. I won't lose you. You're what I live for."

We don't say a word. I am glad that we have this time, but now I have to be the leader that I'm supposed to be.

I can't stay here any longer. It would be too tempting to forget my duty. "I have to go to bed." I crawl off his lap. "I need rest. I need to be able to think clearly tomorrow."

He stands up, still holding onto the fingers of my hand. "We'll figure this out. See you tomorrow." He pulls me close for one last kiss and then he walks out ahead of me. "Night, Darrell."

Darrell is obviously startled when Riley walks off. Darrell says, "I wouldn't say anything if you two spent the night together."

I pat Darrell's shoulder as I watch Riley disappear into the night. "Darrell, I can't deal with that right now. I have a week to save the world."

The next morning, Gretel and Colt busy themselves making breakfast in the kitchen. Moving together as they make coffee and pull croissants out of the oven, they are never more than an arm's length from each other. Gretel eyes are swollen as if she might have been crying most of the night. She and Colt have bags under their eyes. I don't think they got much sleep. I know that my face probably mirrors theirs.

Princess Kamea bounces in. She is as carefree as an autumn leaf skipping its way off a tree and down the rolling hills. I feel a touch of jealousy about her carefree nature. She is in the middle of a worldwide war, but because of her royal status, she is completely sheltered from its horrors. Soon after, Tury arrives carrying Prince Ross.

Gretel and I help Tury fix the two royals a bit of breakfast. When the young ones finally settle, Gretel takes a sip of coffee. "Where's the ambassador?"

Tury fusses with the bib around the prince's neck. "He left out last night. Said he was going to find Paisley and Colt." She takes the bib off the boy, straightens it, and reties it. "He never came back."

"What do you mean he never came back? He's been gone all night?" I swallow a bite of toast.

Tury nods as she pushes Princess Kamea up to the table and places a plate of breakfast in front of her.

"Where could he be?" Colt puts his coffee cup down on the table.

"I'm not sure, but we need to find out." I scan the room. "Darrell can't be far away. I'll head over the radio building. Colt, check with the rest of our security detail. Gretel, check the lab and see if he possibly went there to work for the night."

Gretel smiles a half grin. "Look at you barking orders. You would think that you ran the place." We share a nervous laugh, and then we both abruptly stop. No time for brevity in this horrible situation.

Our half-eaten breakfast is tossed in the garbage while cups and plates are placed in the sink. The children giggle and squeal the entire time watching us run around. Tury attempts to quiet them to no avail.

Gretel and Colt take off in different directions, and I head over to the radio room with my shadow, Darrell, in hot pursuit.

Riley trots along beside us and snuggles my scarf tighter around my neck. "It's cold out here."

"Have you been here all night?" I ask.

He nods. "I know I can't come in, but I ran home and got a change of clothes. Darrell let me share his room. A blanket on the floor is all I need. I wanted to make sure that you were protected."

Darrell moves quickly to my other side. "Right now, two bodyguards can't hurt."

I have to agree with them and am very happy to see Riley. We three make haste to our destination. I walk in with Riley. Darrell stays outside. The room is empty except for the lone operator, Thomas, monitoring the radio.

"Hope you got a little sleep." I pull off my scarf, not waiting for a comment. "Any more news or broadcasts?"

Thomas flips a few pages on a notepad that sits on the table beside him. "A lot of chatter." He flips through his notes and then he sighs. "Do you really want to hear this?"

"Probably not." I plop down in the chair. "But lay it on me anyway."

Riley pulls up a few chairs in anticipation of Gretel, Colt, and others who will be joining us.

The messages center around the demand for my and Colt's immediate surrender. The quotes range from simple requests for us to turn ourselves in to demands that we be locked up for our atrocities committed toward humankind with the re-release of the virus. There is not one message in our support. Riley sits silent, occasionally reaching out to rub my shoulder.

A tear escapes my eye. I'm hated. What would I do without Riley?

Thomas reaches out and pats my hand. "I warned you, the opinions are brutal."

"What about you, Thomas?" I wipe my cheek. "How do you feel about us?"

"I'm just the radio operator." He shifts uncomfortably in the chair. "I'm not qualified to comment."

Riley stands and stretches. "Don't make him answer that, Paisley. He's right, he's not qualified."

"You're wrong, Riley." I slap the notebook. "Thomas is more qualified than the rest of them. He knows me."

Thomas blurts out. "I think you and Colt should turn yourselves in and prove your innocence."

Riley cringes. But Thomas is right, there really is no other choice.

Gretel and Colt come through the door and bring with them a blast of cold air that flutters the pages on Thomas's notebook. Gretel shivers and then pushes the door against the wind. She claps her palms together and blows in them for warmth. "The ambassador's not in the lab."

Chair legs scrape against the floor as Colt scoots one out for Gretel to sit in and slides into another. "I asked all around. Or at least to the people who are awake. Not one person has seen him since last night."

"The ambassador?" Thomas flips a couple of pages back on the notebook. "He was here earlier. Wait a minute." He turns two more pages and then holds a piece of paper out to me. "Yes here it is. He sent a message out."

Colt leans forward. "What did it say?"

I read aloud: "This is Ambassador Grayson. The emperor is a liar. I am proof of that. I plan to travel to Hamburg and negotiate the release of my son Oliver as well as the other two leaders, Captain Via and Lieutenant Drake. There is no need to involve Paisley and Colt. I am the true leader of the resistance. They are innocent and this has all been a ploy to find me." I read the words in disbelief. What has my father done?

"Why would he do that?" Gretel shakes her head. "His job here is so important. I need him. The world needs him to keep developing the antidote." She holds her hands up and shakes her head. "I don't understand."

Colt hugs his wife's shoulders. "I'm sure he didn't think it through. He was just trying to save Paisley and me. Don't worry. We'll make it right."

"We have to go to Hamburg now." I slam down the notebook. "We must save them."

The lights on the radio board start flashing. Thomas perks up and scoots into the table pen in hand, ready to take notation. "Another message is coming through."

It is the emperor's voice. "Ambassador, if you are listening we will await your arrival."

Thomas drops his pen. We sit silently as the emperor continues spewing his lies. "We're so relieved to hear that the ambassador is alive. How wonderful! We look forward to reuniting him with his son. The resistance's efforts to quiet this man were unsuccessful. I know what the ambassador said. I have followed the chatter and the resistance is trying to use him to confuse you."

More of the emperor's lies follow. "Good citizens, you know what the truth is and the truth is that Paisley and Colt are the number one enemies of the world. If any of you know where they are, please let any Merc know. You will be rewarded with treasures and your station in life will be elevated to a level that your heart cannot imagine. Help us take back our world from these monsters. We will report as soon as our beloved ambassador is safely back in our hands. Power to the world. Stomp out the resistance. Signing off Emperor Richard."

"What now?" Riley places his hand on mine. "I don't see how this is not going to be a bloodbath."

Thomas hands me his notebook. He says, "I hate to be the bearer of bad news. But even if we wanted to fight the emperor's regime and obliterate the Mercs, we are losing support everywhere."

I flip through the pages of comments Thomas has written since last night.

Thomas says, "I count at least three strong holds in three different parts of the world that have fallen. There have been reports of resistance supporters putting down their arms and returning to their villages."

"If it keeps going this way," Colt cuts his eyes over to Gretel, "there will be no resistance to fight for."

"We have no choice." I stand and square my shoulders. "We must go and turn ourselves in, and hope that the emperor will release everyone else." I pat Gretel on the shoulder. "I see no other way."

Riley jumps up and embraces me. "There has to be something else we can do." My cheeks flush as he hugs me in front of everyone. I am surprised by the open show of affection. I wrap my arms around his waist and bury my head in his shoulder for a moment.

"You're right, Paisley." Colt slams his fists on the table. "We must turn ourselves in. Let's log all of the information about the resistance. We need to make note of where the troops are and where the weapons are stashed. We have to find out what pockets of the resistance have fallen because of Merc intervention or because they have given up. We must know what we're up against before going to Hamburg."

"Wait a minute, Colt." Riley releases his embrace of me. "I'm not going to fight you or Paisley about turning yourselves in anymore. But give yourselves every chance to come out of this unscathed. Please be smart about it. You need to wait until all of the leaders of the world get to Hamburg. If you go too soon, then the emperor can murder you and blame it on the resistance or an accident."

"But what will happen to the ambassador, Oliver, Lieutenant Drake, and Captain Via while we wait to turn ourselves in?" I shake my head. "No, the safest thing for us to do for them is to go now."

Colt places a hand on each of my arms and turns me to face him. "Riley is right. We have to make it a public spectacle. It's the only way to have any chance at a fair trial."

"None of this is fair. Do you really think any of this is fair?" I jerk out of his grasp. "All of these lies. The emperor's evil deeds turned back on us as if we were the ones who committed those heinous crimes. How is any of this possibly fair? Why would anyone think the emperor would be fair now?"

Gretel drapes her arm around my shoulder. "You're right Paisley. The emperor is a liar and a cheat, but that is even more of a reason to make sure there is a public trial. The eyes of the world *must* be watching. It's the only chance you and Colt have. It's the only chance for the truth to come out. Don't you see that?"

Gretel squeezes me again. "I know you, sister. I know you want to march head on and take on the emperor. But not this time. You need to pause, take a breath. Rest and make a plan. Please."

"She's right. Listen to her." Riley clasps my hand. "We'll help you and Colt make a plan. It's the right way, the only way."

Darrell joins us now and holds out his palm. One by one, I along with Thomas, Gretel, Colt, and Riley join hands. We whisper. "Power to the resistance." We say it, but the fire is not there. If we hope to defeat the emperor, we must get our passion and determination back. We will definitely need luck to make it happen. I pull out the four-leaf clover and twirl it in my fingers.

Colt and I spend the day updating the map. It doesn't look good. Our forces are dwindling. Winning seems impossible. With the ambassador heading back into enemy hands, the emperor will now have a monopoly on manufacturing the cure. My father's brain wasn't thinking about the cure. He's my dad. He

217

did it for me, Oliver, the little prince, and the princess. He did it for his family. An unselfish act. A reckless act, but an understandable one. My father unconditionally loves his family. Of that, I have no doubt.

That night we gather for the broadcast once again. Gretel and Colt sit close to each other. Darrell stands in the back of the room. Riley slides a chair near me. Thomas mans the radio board. I dread the news. It will be bad, I'm sure of it.

We don't have to wait long. Lights flash and the emperor's voice sounds. "Good evening fellow citizens. Tonight, I share wonderful news. The ambassador has come back to us."

The sound of clapping hands in the background of the transmission is followed by more of the emperor's voice. "He is standing here with me and will be given an opportunity to speak in a few minutes. The ambassador and his long lost son have been reunited. It is a great day for the right side, our side. Those evil resistance fighters have lost many of their strong holds in the countries of South America..."

Thomas flips a page and starts writing.

The emperor continues, "We have taken control of the camps in Canada and half of the resistance bases in the United States, all in Asia and one in Europe. Don't

218

worry my friends there will be no place for the heathens to hide. Paisley and Colt still cower like the cowards that they are, and I have faith that they will be caught and brought to justice very soon."

The emperor clears his throat. "Our government, the one and only true government, sanctioned by the Consortium and led by me, your emperor, will now begin the manufacture and distribution of the cure. For those who have not had an opportunity to be inoculated, no fear, this small vial represents life and peace of mind, and will be available to you by the week's end. Go to any local stores backed by the Consortium of the World and you will receive the cure. There is a small service charge to pay for our costs. If you have no money, we will take food or other valuables as trade. We have implemented the barter system and all of you will be able to get the boosters that are required to keep the immunity..."

Leaning in close to Gretel, I whisper, "Booster, do you need boosters?"

"No. He must be working on lessening the dosage to force the need for the booster." She shakes her head. "He's trying to control the people forever."

We listen to the vile emperor's lies. "Boosters need to be taken monthly. If you have no means by which to pay, we will provide opportunities to earn small stipends. Contracts for service will be available for you to sign. You will be able to work off your debt."

Legally binding human trafficking, complete with a signed contract. How horrible! Uncounteds and Undesirables will sign their freedom away in order to obtain an immunity from the virus. It's a guarantee that should be given for free, no strings attached. Emperor Richard must be stopped. My face reddens as heat surges through my body. I force myself to remain calm.

The emperor continues, "We must have Paisley and Colt in custody before the cure will be available."

I can't believe it. It takes all of my self-control not to scream. He's holding the cure from everyone to try to force us to turn ourselves in. He wouldn't have the cure if it wasn't for my father. How could my father been manipulated by this maniac? I put my hand over my heart trying to calm its increasing beats. "Keep yourself together," I tell myself.

The evil man spews more lies. "More good news. Our Oliver has agreed to repair the World Wide Web. Please go and find any old television or computer because communication will soon be restored. Our Oliver is one of a kind. We appreciate him and are so happy he is back on our side."

A few claps are heard over the broadcast before the emperor continues. "We plan to have everything up and running by next Sunday, the first day of the rule of the new Consortium of the World. This is a great day and I am proud to be your leader. I know the people are behind me and that I will be voted to carry on as your leader. Fear not fellow people of the world. Our side, the right side, will win." He takes a breath. "And now for a message from Ambassador Grayson."

My heart leaps when I hear my father's name. He is alive. Of course he is alive, the emperor needs him. He needs him to make the cure. I am sure he is using Oliver to control him and obviously, the emperor is using the ambassador's arrest to control Oliver. How can I hold onto hope?

"I'm here with the emperor, which is true." My father's voice increases my faith. "I have found a cure, which is also correct. My son, Oliver, is here with me, another truth. There is one thing that you don't know. If you and the emperor want me to live because of my connection to the royal family..."

The emperor's voice cuts in. "Stay on script Mr. Ambassador."

My father interrupts, "Oliver and I are alive because we are royals. Isn't that correct, Emperor Richard?"

Colt moves closer to the speaker. "What's he doing?"

Gretel scrunches in close to Colt. "He never does anything without a plan."

Emperor Richard clears his throat. "Of course Ambassador Grayson. The world wants you to live. Royals have immunity from prosecution. No harm will come to you and your son. You are a royal. I, Emperor Richard, and the government promise on the public radio that no harm will come to you or your family."

Unintelligible mumblings follow. The emperor coughs. "There is one piece of disturbing information that I have chosen not to share with the people, but I want to tell you now. Our little prince and princess are missing. In fact, I promise safety for Prince Ross and Princess Kamea if whoever is holding them will release them. I suspect as I have for a while and especially since Ambassador Grayson is alive and does not have them, that a faction of the resistance, maybe Paisley and Colt themselves, are holding our precious young and vulnerable prince and princess."

Emperor Richard spews more evil. "I shudder to think what will happen to them. Please return them unharmed or give us information regarding our young royals' whereabouts. Per usual if you give any information to my government or any of the Mercs, the sanctioned security of this government, you will be amply rewarded."

Riley scratches his head. "This is making no sense. It's as if the ambassador has cut a deal with the emperor. It sounds as if he really is on his side. What does all of this mean?"

"No way." I say aloud. "He would never sell us out."

"Shush!" Gretel hisses.

"I have your promise." My father comes back on the radio. "No harm will come to any of member of my family."

A pause is followed by the emperor's voice. "I give you my word and my word is witnessed by this national audience. No harm will come to any member of your family."

My father comes back on. "Well then I ask for safety for my daughter."

The emperor says, "Of course. I have already told you that. Princess Kamea will always be safe."

"Oh no." I mumble to myself. I know what's coming.

"No." My father says, "My other daughter. I ask for safety for my oldest daughter. The one you seek, Paisley, is my daughter and I can prove it."

The lights blink on and off and the radio goes silent.

Chapter 22

All eyes in the radio room train in on me. I shoot up out of my chair.

"Paisley?" Gretel walks over and stands by me. "I knew you weren't ours, but I didn't realize that the ambassador was your father. When did you find out?"

Colt interrupts, "Wait a minute. Is this true?"

I nod.

Riley slides over close to me. "You could have told me."

"I know." I touch his arm. "I should have told you." I scan the room. "I guess I should have told all of you."

"It's fine. No one is angry. Tell us now." Riley guides me back to my chair. "You're among friends."

Darrell peeks in. "You should probably tell everyone. It seems that the emperor's announcement has been broadcast to the compound via loudspeaker and the message has been heard by all. Rumors are flying. I think maybe you should tell everyone at one time."

"Didn't realize you were doing that, Thomas." Colt glances at Thomas, who is sitting quietly in front of the microphone. "Don't worry. I'm not mad, it's fine. Everyone should know. No secrets."

Colt stands up and taps Thomas's shoulder. "Thomas, go out and pass the message that in thirty minutes Paisley and I will address the troops. Make sure that everyone knows. All should attend."

I put my hands on my hips. "I probably should go talk to Tury and the prince and princess right now. I'll bring them with me."

"Paisley?" Gretel holds her hands on each side of my face. "You want me to go with you?"

"Not right now." I pat her hands. "But I appreciate the gesture." Squeezing her hands, I assure her. "This doesn't change anything. You're still my sister." We hug tightly.

Gretel says, "I know. Sisters now and forever. Sisters always." She releases the hug.

Before I leave her, I glance at Darrell. "We need to go the castle." Darrell opens the door wide.

I get to the exit and turn around. "Riley, would you mind going with me? I'd like to have you there when I tell the children."

Riley beams. "Of course, whatever you want." As soon as he reaches me, he kisses me. It's a small kiss, but a kiss just the same.

Riley pulls back and says, "No more secrets."

The public kiss announces to the people in the room that we are together. It's liberating.

Telling the children is easier than I think. Not sure if they understand, they don't ask many questions, but I feel better. Having Riley there helps. If I could only figure out a way to win this war while rescuing the prisoners held by the emperor, including my father and brother, all would be right with the world.

Did Oliver listen to the broadcast? What did he think of my father's confession? Did he ever consider the possibility I was his sister? My questions will have to wait. I must address my compound now.

As I arrive, I hear whispers from faceless mouths in the front of the crowd. I have lied to them. How will I ever be able to get them to trust me again?

Colt introduces me. "Here is Paisley to explain the ambassador's message."

I fold my hands in front of me trying to look as demure and honest as I can. "I want to tell you the truth about what is going on. I know that I have not always been honest. For those who do not know, this morning the ambassador revealed that I am indeed his daughter."

Gasps from the crowd cause me to pause a few seconds before continuing. "Oliver and I are the ambassador's children from his first marriage. First me, a few years before, and Oliver after the virus broke out. Through a series of unfortunate circumstances, my family was separated. I was lucky enough to have been rescued and cared for by Gretel..." My eyes lock with Gretel's. "...and her family for the years following the virus quarantine. I never questioned that I was a member of that family."

Gretel pipes in. "You *are* a member of my family."

I smile. "Of course I am. When Colt and I stowed away on the ship in an attempt to rescue Gretel and my mom we ran into the ambassador. During a routine blood check, he discovered it was my blood that provided the key for the cure..."

"Your blood is the blood we use for the cure?" Someone in the back shouts.

"Yes, good citizen. It's my blood. This is when the ambassador realized who I was and revealed himself to me. He told me that he was my father. He begged me to keep it a secret for fear that the king would have me killed."

Most heads nod in the crowd signaling that they were in agreement with Ambassador Grayson's choice to keep me a secret.

I continue, "My father explained that the virus was discovered many years ago. He made a serum that would provide an immunity for the disease. He saw no need to advise the distribution of the cure to everyone because the virus was just an idea. A couple of cells in the Petri dish. There was no need for a mass inoculation and it was deemed inappropriate to scare the world by forcing injections on the masses. He knew the inoculation was safe so he gave himself the cure and he injected me and my mother who was pregnant with my brother."

Colt moves a little closer to me to show support.

"After the virus infected the world my father lost me and my mother." I take a breath. "While searching for us, he found my infant brother, but was told his wife was lost. He couldn't find me. When he went back to the lab, the cure and all of the machines had been moved."

"I know about the machines," Colt interjects. "The ambassador told me it was unclear where those machines were moved. Years later he found a working machine during his travels to Africa."

Colt motions to his wife. "Gretel, why don't you explain about the DNA since you are the scientist?"

Gretel jumps up on the platform beside us and addresses the crowd. "After he travelled to Africa, he needed the perfect DNA. His DNA contained a flaw and he would not be able to manufacture the cure from his own blood. He discovered the same problem with all of the donors. He found out that he had to have a female donor. That perfect donor turned out to be my sister, Paisley. That is all I can report about the DNA. Now my sister, Paisley, will tell you anything else she thinks she needs to share."

"Thanks for filling that in. See there are things that I did not know. We are not the bad people the emperor is making us out to be. But I am indeed the daughter of the ambassador, the sister of Oliver, and the half-sister of the young royals, Prince Ross and Princess Kamea. I am sorry that I have kept you in the dark but I promise not to do that anymore."

I glance at Riley. "In keeping with wanting to tell you everything, I need Riley to come to the front."

Riley slowly rises and joins me. "What are you doing?"

"In the spirit of not hiding anything. I need to tell you one more thing." I hook my arm through Riley's. "Riley and I are together. So for those of you who might see us holding hands, I mean we are…"

"Okay, Paisley." Colt pops up in front. "You are entitled to a private life. Who you choose to spend your time with is entirely up to you. I am sure that this is more information than this group needs to know. You do have some privacy." He scans the group. "Questions?"

A voice from the back yells, "Yeah, how long have Riley and Paisley been a couple?"

Colt claps his hands together. "Any question about the virus or Paisley being the ambassador's daughter." He swings his finger as if he is polling the crowd. "Seeing no hands, let's move along with the problem at hand. Paisley and I are going to be turning ourselves in to the authorities of the Consortium of the World on Sunday."

Gasps break the silence. A few loud "no's" are heard throughout the crowd.

"Colt and I have to turn ourselves in. We have to trust the system." I yell, "Truth will win out. We have no other choice."

The crowd quiets and Colt continues, "We need to figure out some contingency plans for the compound."

Leaning close to Colt's ear, I whisper, "I know my emergency plans for my half. What I want to do. Do you?"

"Obviously." Colt points to Gretel.

Looking out at the group, I announce, "If Colt and I are found guilty and sentenced to death we want to continue Aunt Sandra's refuge for those downtrodden and for the Undesirables and Uncounteds."

I motion for Riley. "Riley will be in charge of my half of Aunt Sandra's farm. He will hold it for Prince Ross and Princess Kamea who will each own half as soon as they come of age. There will be a provision for Tury and Riley to have their own piece of land."

The crowd groans.

"Might not work." Riley leans over and whispers in my ear. "I'll be going with you, I might not make it back."

What a horrible thought! I hate to think about it, but I can't let the children be without a guardian. So I continue, "If something happens to Riley, Tury is in charge and then Thomas."

"Don't go!" A soldier yells.

"Finished?" Colt joins me. I nod and he walks in front of the group. "My half will be in the hands of my wife, Gretel. She will complete the ambassador's work."

A young mother cries, "What will we do without you?"

"You can't leave us." A teenage boy hollers.

The crowd drowns us out now with their objections.

"Quiet!" Colt and I yell in unison and the crowd goes silent.

"Look, people," I say. "We don't plan to die. This isn't a suicide mission. We plan to win this thing. We want to come back." I grab Colt's wrist and raise our arms up in the air. "Power to the resistance!" I yell, emphasizing each word. "We must not let Aunt Sandra's legacy die. Aunt Sandra's legacy must live on. No matter what. Accept our decisions. Do it for Aunt Sandra."

A young boy stands up and claps. One by one, the crowd claps. I am moved by the ovation of reverence. I choke back the tears.

The great Aunt Sandra is truly a hard act to follow.

Chapter 23

Only a few days remain before we must depart for Hamburg. Lots of work to complete and plans to make. Colt and I work feverishly sending couriers to each of the standing factions of resistance to update them on our plan.

We urgently ask them to make sure to get the cure to all and to watch out for the weak in case Colt and I are killed. We encourage the troops to remain diligent in their fight for freedom with or without us.

I try to spend as much time as I can with Riley and the prince and princess. This may be the last time I see them. I want to make happy memories. The thought of not being with Riley makes me full of empty. I spend my nights in the children's room and Riley stays there with me. I'm cuddled with a blanket on the floor and he is draped over a chair. It fills my heart with joy to see him when I fall asleep and when I wake up.

Gretel and Colt spend all of their time together and are not apart for a minute. I can't tell where one starts and the other begins. I'm not sure if my sister will survive if something happens to Colt. But that is something I don't have the luxury of time to worry about now in the middle of this fight for our lives and democracy.

We make no formal announcement of our exact time for departure. It'll be better that way. No pomp and circumstance. We need to be mission ready, heart, soul, and mind. No distractions. In the wee hours of Saturday morning, we make our move. The darkness of the night will hide us from the enemy.

Colt struggles at the thought of leaving Gretel behind. At least Riley will be with me should Colt and I get the death penalty. Is my father still alive? Oliver? The World Wide Web is running, a sure clue that Oliver is still alive. I hold onto hope that I will see my father and brother again.

What about Lieutenant Drake and Captain Via? Could Captain Via really be my birth mother? What if I'm right and she has already been executed? Sadness enters my soul and tears well. Stop thinking that way, I tell myself. I must be sharp if I'm to answer questions from the tribunal of the Consortium of the World and convince them of my truthfulness in order to save mine and Colt's life as well as the scores of innocents caught in the middle of this battle.

The night travel leading up to the Sunday morning is foggy. I'm scared. More afraid than I've ever been. So many people are depending on me. I must keep my mind on other things, so I concentrate on Riley, the best thing that has ever happened to me.

Sunday at noon, Colt, Riley, Darrell and I ride down the streets of Hamburg amid scores of people lining the streets.

At the end of the street, Emperor Richard is perched upon a makeshift throne on a second story balcony of the tallest building. "Paisley and Colt, are you here to turn yourselves in?"

Colt and I step in front of Darrell and Riley. Riley holds tight to my hand. I let my arm stretch behind me, afraid to let go of him. I squeeze his hand for strength. I shout to the emperor and to the masses. "Emperor Richard, please keep your promise and let the prisoners go."

The emperor stands and glances from side to side. "I'll keep my promise." Guards open a gate. A flood of people move out. I recognize some. Some hobble, all are dirty. They are afraid, but free.

Colt commands to the recently released. "Leave this place quickly." He looks at the emperor. "We would like your solemn oath that you will not harm or capture these people again."

The emperor lowers his head in a slight bow. "I promise."

We watch the parade of people pass us. The group mainly consists of children with a few crippled adults guiding them along. They mouth "thank you" and cry, while smiling and holding onto each other. It is a few minutes before they disappear at the end of the street, scattering everywhere. I hold onto Riley.

Not seeing the captives I expected to see, I inquire to the emperor. "What about Lieutenant Drake and Captain Via?"

The emperor glances at a Merc guarding another gate. The gate clangs as it slowly rises and guards pull out a blindfolded Captain Via and Lieutenant Drake. They stumble as they are led out.

I yell, "Captain, Lieutenant are you okay?"

Lieutenant Drake calls out, "Paisley, is that you?"

"Yes. You are to be set free."

The captain shouts out, "What did you have to trade for us?"

Colt sums it up. "A chance to tell the truth in front of the world."

Lieutenant Drake yells. "Sounds like a good trade."

A Merc slams Captain Via and Lieutenant Drake to the dirt on their knees and their blindfolds are removed.

"Wait!" I shout. "You promised they would be set free."

The emperor gives a sly grin. "If you can prove your innocence, all will be set free."

He will always be a liar. We sacrificed ourselves on the promise of a liar.

Is hope for peace and freedom for our world lost forever?

Chapter 24

"**W**here are my father and brother?"

The emperor shouts. "Who are you to ask questions? You are a secret daughter. He didn't know about you until a few months ago. I will not listen to you." He stands and raises his arms outward to the masses. "Citizens, I submit to you that Paisley is not a true royal. She committed treason. She is a traitor. She should be reviled, not saved. She is the scum of the earth."

A few "boos" escape the mouths of the audience. I do have some who are on my side, some support. But not enough, I fear.

"Citizens! Citizens!" Emperor Richard adjusts his crown. "I know who the real royals are and you do too.

I will keep our true royals safe. For you, my people, I will show you that the ambassador and his son are not harmed."

There is a large screen set up to the side of the emperor. It turns to black and beeps. The images of my father and brother come into view.

"See, Citizens. I have kept my promise. The ambassador and his son are completely unharmed. The members of the Consortium of the World will view these proceedings via the television." The emperor points to various cameras mounted around the balcony and aimed toward the street where we are being held captive.

"This is a public trial. We will begin." The emperor grasps both sides of the collars of his robe and paces back and forth across his stage bellowing to the cameras. "People and members of the Consortium of the World, I have spent the last two weeks gathering evidence about these four conspirators. Paisley, Colt, Lieutenant Drake, and Captain Via."

The emperor nods slightly to the Merc holding the lieutenant and the captain. The Merc jerks them to their feet and pushes them next to Colt and me. Another Merc pulls Riley back and our hands are forced apart. Riley and Darrell are held at gunpoint by Mercs behind Colt and me.

The emperor continues, "I sent packets to the members of the consortium two days ago. They took their time and painstakingly read over the evidence. This morning, I visited and gathered votes from each member of the Consortium of the World and have personally counted those votes."

"After tallying those votes, I have a verdict." He rolls out a parchment. "I will read the verdict. It is the consensus of this panel of the Consortium of the World that these four: Paisley, Colt, Lieutenant Drake, and Captain Via be sentenced to immediate death for the charge of treason. I have also attained the signature of the ambassador that he too agrees that his own daughter be sentenced to death because of her traitorous nature and her continued threat to our way of life."

My vision blurs. Everything spins. Colt and the Lieutenant catch me before I fall. The other three stand steadfast. Colt shouts, "Don't we get to defend?"

What am I going to do? I've let everyone down. Our world will never be free. My heart sinks as I stare at the screen with the image of my father. I cannot believe that my father would ever betray me.

Wait, something is wrong with the feed on the monitor. Why is my father repeating the same movement on the television screen? Neither he nor Oliver has changed actions since they came on the screen. I focus for a minute before I realize it's on a loop. It's the same each time. What does that mean?

Have they already been killed?

If they have, then all hope is lost.

"No!" My father's voice pierces through the speakers. The screen above the emperor morphs into a different picture. Every one quiets.

The image is that of Oliver, my father, and the leaders of the Consortium of the World.

"Emperor Richard is lying!" My father addresses the crowd through the mounted monitors. "He did not meet with any of the members of the Consortium of the World. No votes were gathered. They have been held captive just as I was held captive. We managed to break free."

My father takes in a big breath. "We managed to keep our escape secret from the emperor using the expertise of my son, Oliver, through fake images displayed on the security monitors. We also have found help through resistance sympathizers who have helped us keep up this ruse."

My father speaks quickly. "I know that you thought you were going to witness a public execution of traitors, but I have been meeting with the leaders of the world and we have come up with a better solution for our world. Hijacking this media blitz is the only way I knew to deliver this message. I represent not only myself, but the leaders of the world. Every region is represented. I am here to shed light on what is really going on. Please listen to these leaders."

One by one the elders of each country tell of the atrocities that have happened because of the virus and subsequent quarantine. Each horrible account of the atrocities committed in their respective countries is followed by gasps from the crowd. After sharing, each leader publically endorses the new democratic constitution.

The emperor enlists help from the Mercs by his side and scrambles the whole time the leaders are speaking, trying to no avail to find the cut off for the feed. His desperation grows with each failure to shut off the broadcast.

The ambassador says, "We have spent our time huddled together hashing out the fine print. Even though it is a document, it is an ever-changing one. We need to reestablish communication, stabilize the farms, distribute the food, and make sure everyone is given the cure. If the correct dosage is given, there is no need for a booster. The need for a booster is another lie spread by Emperor Richard."

Our captive group watches along with everyone else. My hope increases with each word. Finally giving up on shutting off the broadcast from his perch, the emperor disappears from the balcony. What can he do now? Everyone knows about his treachery. Maybe the emperor will run away. I hope he leaves and is never seen again.

"Fellow citizens, no one from the resistance was trying to reintroduce the virus." My father drops his head. "Since you must know the truth and the whole truth, I have a confession to make. When I was working for the military, I was contracted to develop a machine that would take the DNA out of blood and then be able to replace it with another DNA."

My father stares intently into the monitor. "Unfortunately, I was paired with other scientists who were contracted to make a virus. The virus was to be a bioterrorist weapon that would be used on parts of the world considered enemies. That virus caused the first outbreak. The bioterrorist weapon that should have never been developed in the first place almost wiped out the entire population. Because I was involved in that horrible mistake from the very beginning stages, I have made it my life's work to find and develop a cure. I succeeded thanks entirely to the DNA of my daughter, Paisley. "

"I propose," he begins, spreading his arms wide, "we stop this war and get behind this democratic process..."

A deafening, loud bang resonates from the television and I watch in horror as my father slumps over. The crowd screams as blood pours from his head. Oliver cradles my father. The emperor, his face mad with rage, is wrestled to the ground by the Consortium of the World's new security team. A gun is wrenched out of his hand.

The emperor screams. "Take them men."

More men with guns rush the room and surround the Mercs.

One of the Consortium of the World representatives announces, "The Mercs now are under arrest by the Consortium of the World security. They no longer work for you." He says to the emperor. "You have just been ousted and stripped of power."

The new security personnel quickly lead the handcuffed emperor and his Mercs out of the building.

The crowd cheers. The Mercs responsible for us release their hold, fling off their caps and jackets, and attempt to escape by blending in with the crowd. They are quickly rounded up by the new security. Riley wastes no time getting to my side, pulling me close.

The screen goes black. I look at Riley. "I need to find my father."

"Does anyone know where the ambassador is?" Colt yells to the new security men now surrounding us.

"I do." A security man standing by Riley holds out his hand. "I'm John. At your service. Follow me."

Riley shakes John's hand. The lieutenant, the captain, Riley, Colt, Darrell and I all follow John. He leads us into the building. We make our way quickly to the room that was showing on the screen earlier. The room where my father is. Inside, sobs echo throughout the room. Members of the Consortium of the World and the new security surround my father.

Forcing my way to my father's side. I drop to my knees. "Father?" I take his hand.

He is bleeding and Oliver shakes his head. I realize that my father doesn't have long. His eyes brim with tears when he spies me. He reaches up. "My sweet girl." Then the look in his eyes changes as he looks over my shoulder and his face lights up. "Oh, Olivia. My beautiful Olivia."

"Why is he calling me Olivia?" I squeeze his hand and turn around. Captain Via and Lieutenant Drake stand behind us.

"Yes, Ross, it's me." Captain Via squats down beside my father and grasps his other hand. "I'm sorry. I thought you were dead at first. I didn't realize you and Oliver were still alive until you had already married the queen. I thought you were better off not knowing I was still alive."

A tear runs down my mother's cheek. "I thought you and Oliver were better off where you were." She sniffs in another tear. "I'm sorry I should have told you."

"Don't cry, my wife." My father wipes a tear from my mother's cheek and reaches his hand toward Oliver. Struggling to make a sound, he finally grunts out. "Oliver, this is your mother. This is my family. We all made it. We're here together. I'm so happy."

Tears stream down my face. My father is dying. We finally find each other and now my father is going to die.

"Olivia." My father whispers as my mother leans in. "I always loved you. I always will."

My mother nods. "I know, me too, my love." She leans down and kisses his forehead. His grip loosens from my hand.

My father is gone.

Chapter 25

Everything that is me hurts. My heart, my soul, my body. I miss my father so much I can't function for a few weeks. I am taken to the infirmary and while I recuperate all of the specifics of the new world order are voted on.

A new constitution is drafted. Lots of compromises. The whole world will be ruled by a democratic vote. A first. A great start for world peace. In a way, I'm glad to have missed it all.

Riley never leaves my side although he and I don't speak much at first. I'm not strong enough. As time passes, a numbness takes over and I don't hurt as much. After a few weeks, all that is left is a hole in my being that my father once occupied.

I am glad to have Captain Via, my mother, and Oliver, my new found brother. The two of them are great, visiting many times. We share stories and with the connection of my father to link our past and the young prince and princess to connect our future, we are well on our way to building a long-lasting relationship. I love my newly found family. I guess in a way it's poetic that on the day I lost one loved one, I gained so many more.

My mother, Captain Via, agrees to work with Lieutenant Drake to travel to each of the countries to set up communication and democratic rule. A United Nations is established and the governments become part of one entity, living in peace. Worldwide distribution of food is established and volunteer fire and police departments are set up in each country. Locals make the specific rules about their products. Barter systems are in place. The virus cure is free. The outlook for total and complete peace is positive.

My brother, Oliver, begins his job to train others in the technology. Even though we had a twelve-year hiatus from technology and communications, the world quickly catches up. Oliver plans to travel the globe.

It is a joyful day when I return to the compound. Tury and my half-brother and half-sister are living happily with me in the castle. It is amazing how resilient children are.

Gretel is busy in the lab and making the Becker Bavarian a home. She surprises Colt and the rest of us with the news that he will be a father come next summer. She'll be a natural mother. I can't wait to spoil my new niece or nephew. Very exciting!

Riley becomes instrumental and an intricate part of running the day to day operations of Aunt Sandra's lands. Riley and I are still dating. When we get older we may marry, but for now, we are taking it one day at a time.

In late spring, I decide to visit my Ferris wheel farm. It's been a long time.

Riding through the countryside, I realize that I'm no longer an "Uncounted."

This moonlit evening, the giant Ferris wheel casts an ominous shadow beckoning to me. Left over from a long forgotten carnival, the rusty, dilapidated wheel remains workable.

The Ferris wheel has been on our farm as long as I can remember. I love it, even though it's rusty, tattered, and the color of a rotten banana peel. Its uniqueness makes it special. I climb into the bottom chair and hit the lever to take my ride. The brisk Bavarian air pricks my face like a hundred needles.

From my perch, I see hints of grass peeking out of the shimmering snow and watch the hills roll into the evening darkness. I'm overcome by a tranquil sense of freedom. My thrilled heart beats and my face flushes.

The creaking interrupts my thoughts as the Ferris wheel slowly begins its ascent. Complete joy surges through me. I spread my arms. I'm finally free. I am a person. I'm not an Uncounted.

I matter.

The End

ABOUT THE AUTHOR

Susan Womble is an award-winning author. Susan Womble lives in Tallahassee, Florida with her family. She is a retired National Board Certified teacher with a career of teaching grades K-12th in the areas of reading, special education, language arts, math, social studies, and the profoundly handicapped. Visit www.susanwomble.com for more information. Contact her at susan.womble@gmail.com

Other Books by Susan Larned Womble

1) **Bloodstone Legacy** ISBN-13: 978-0-9913997-8-5
2) **The Big Wheel** ISBN-13: 978-0-9913977-0-9
3) **Take The Helm** ISBN-13: 978-0-9913977-7-8
4) **Newt's World: Beginnings** ISBN: 978-0-9913977-1-6
5) **Newt's World: Internal Byte** ISBN: 978-0-9913977-2-3

6) **Newt's World: Beginnings Workbook Teacher's Edition** ISBN: 978-0-9913977-3-0

7) **Newt's World: Beginnings Workbook Student's Edition** ISBN: 978-0-9913977-4-7

8) **Newt's World: Internal Byte Workbook Teacher's Edition** ISBN: 978-0-9913977-5-4

9) **Newt's World: Internal Byte Workbook Student's Edition** ISBN: 978-0-9913977-6-1

Awards and Notables

- **Gold Medal Florida Book Award in children's literature 2008 for "Newt's World: Beginnings"**
- **Newt's World Beginnings on 2009, 2010, 2011, 2012, 2013, 2014 Just Read Florida Recommended Reading Lists**

www.ingramcontent.com/pod-product-compliance
Lightning Source LLC
Chambersburg PA
CBHW030914120626
46554CB00001B/143